THE CASE OF THE
PIGGY BANK
THIEF

Read all the First Kids Mysteries

The Case of the Rock 'n' Roll Dog

The Case of the Diamond Dog Collar

The Case of the Ruby Slippers

The Case of the Piggy Bank Thief

The Case of the Dinosaur Egg

4

THE CASE OF THE
PIGGY BANK
THIEF

MARTHA FREEMAN

Holiday House / New York

ACKNOWLEDGMENTS

The author acknowledges the generous assistance of Karen Lee, curator of the National Numismatic Collection of the Smithsonian Institution, and graduate student Evan Cooney. I am also grateful to Dr. Richard G. Doty, director of the collection and author of eight books and hundreds of articles on coins, money, and collecting, including the invaluable and engaging *America's Money, America's Story: A Chronicle of American Numismatic History* (Whitman Publishing, 2008). Finally, I'd like to thank my friend Aracyn Etie and her search dog, Gauge, who lost me in the woods and then found me again.

Library of Congress Cataloging-in-Publication Data
Freeman, Martha, 1956-
The case of the piggy bank thief / Martha Freeman. — 1st ed.
p. cm. — (First kids mystery ; #4)
Summary: Seven-year-old Tessa and ten-year-old Cammie, the first female president's daughters, investigate when Tessa's piggy bank goes missing and gold is discovered on the White House grounds.
ISBN 978-0-8234-2517-4 (hardcover)
1. White House (Washington, D.C.)—Juvenile fiction. [1. White House (Washington, D.C.)—Fiction. 2. Presidents—Family—Fiction. 3. Sisters—Fiction. 4. Coins—Fiction. 5. Lost and found possessions—Fiction. 6. Washington (D.C.)—Fiction. 7. Mystery and detective stories.] I. Title.
PZ7.F87496Caq 2012
[Fic]—dc23
2011051276

ISBN 978-0-8234-2916-5 (paperback)

For my friend and coffee date Rick Bryant,
who gives me all my best ideas

THE CASE OF THE
PIGGY BANK
THIEF

CHAPTER ONE

MORE than a million people come to my house every year.

And on Saturday, it felt like they all showed up at once.

Usually my family and I stay out of the way when visitors are downstairs, but sometimes that's just not possible—like when our big, furry, too-energetic dog is out of control, chasing I'm-not-sure-what on the ground floor, which is where tourists enter the White House.

Since January, when my mom got to be president, the White House is where my family lives.

Tessa, my sister, kept yelling at our dog, "Hoo-Hoo-Hooligan! *Stop!*", which was pointless because when Hooligan gets going, the only thing that stops him is a rock wall or a yummy smell.

Up till a few minutes earlier, things had been pretty normal. Tessa had gone to ballet, and I had gone to soccer, like we always do on Saturday morning. Then we came home and changed into grotty old clothes. That's because that afternoon we were supposed to go do something cool—help some college students working on an archeology dig out by the pool in our backyard, the South Lawn.

Meanwhile, it was almost lunchtime when Jeremy—he's the tallest Secret Service agent, plus he has this really deep voice—pounded on our bedroom door with his radio going crazy: "Mayday on the ground floor! Urgent action required—send Fireball and Fussbudget! Someone's got to control this dog!"

Fireball, if you're wondering, is Tessa. Fussbudget is me. If the Secret Service has to protect you, they give you your own special code name.

The White House is big, 132 rooms, not counting the two wings where the offices are. You can move through it pretty fast, though, if you know the shortcuts. Tessa and I went from the second floor to the ground floor in two minutes, and there we found all those White House visitors scrambling, scattering, and screaming.

You would've thought Hooligan was Godzilla or something.

Tessa shook her head. "People, people, people—can't you all just simmer down?"

But I felt bad.

Maybe you've never visited the White House, but how it works is, you have to make a reservation way in advance, then wait in a long line at the East Entrance, and you can't bring in a purse, or a camera, or a bottle of water, or anything.

Once you're inside, you pass through the Garden

Room to the East Wing colonnade, which has the Jacqueline Kennedy Garden on one side and the movie theater on the other. From there you enter the ground floor of the residence part of the White House, and you go by the Library and the Vermeil Room, then turn right and go upstairs to the State Floor.

All the time, you have to stay behind ropes, and there are Secret Service officers to answer questions and make sure you obey the rules.

Anyway, Tessa was worried about Hooligan, but I was thinking how these visitors had gone to so much trouble for their White House tour, and here came our dog—ruining everything.

"Sorry! Sorry! Sorry!" I said as we bumped and dodged, trying to catch Hooligan. "Excuse us! He usually doesn't hurt anybody. I am so sorry...."

You can probably imagine that with so many people and such a big dog, it was pretty loud down there, and then—above it all—I heard something shrill and unexpected: *Twee-twee-twee!*

Tessa grabbed my arm. "Is that Humdinger?"

I was going to say, "Can't be," but a flash of yellow feathers proved me wrong.

Oh, swell.

Now the White House visitors had two rampaging pets to worry about: dog on the ground and canary in the air.

"There he goes again!" Tessa pointed. Humdinger's not much of a flier, so he was using the chandeliers to make progress, short-hop fluttering from one to the next.

Charlotte, the Secret Service agent who had radioed for us, was stationed at the bottom of the main stairs that lead up to the State Floor, and Hooligan was almost in her tackle range when I guess he heard canary wings, because he stopped and looked around before sitting himself down and howling: *"Awh-roohr!"*

Then he repeated his song for anyone who'd missed the first performance.

I stumbled up and grabbed his collar. "Gotcha!"

And Tessa threw her arms around his neck. "Poor puppy, were you scared?"

After that, Mr. Ng came up behind us and reached for Hooligan's leash. Mr. Ng watches Hooligan on weekends, and he told us what had happened. They were on the South Lawn when Hooligan did his frenzy thing—lunged forward, thumped his paws, sprang high in the air and spun so fast he turned blurry.

Tangled up in leash, Mr. Ng had a choice: He could either let go or fall flat. He picked let go—wouldn't you?—and the second he did, Hooligan charged through an open door.

"I don't know what came over him," said Mr. Ng.

"I do," said Tessa. "He heard the Humdinger alarm system."

It was quieter in the hall now, with Hooligan under control, and Tessa elbowed me. "Cammie, you have to say something. Everybody's looking at you."

"I think they're looking at you," I said.

"Maybe. But I'm only a second grader."

I tried not to think how much I hated doing this, stood

up and turned to face the crowd. "Uh...hi, everybody. My name's Cameron Parks, and—"

Tessa whispered, "They *know* that."

I frowned. "Do you want to talk?"

Tessa pressed her lips together; some people laughed, and I felt better. "My sister and I...uh...and our dog... uh...and our canary are all really sorry," I said. "So we hope you'll go ahead and have a really nice day of sightseeing here in our nation's capital."

"Also," Tessa added, "don't forget to vote for our mom!"

This time, practically everybody laughed.

Meanwhile, Mr. Ng wanted to know: "What are we going to do about Humdinger?"

CHAPTER TWO

MR. Ng had asked a good question. Humdinger was still loose, currently perched on a sculpture of Benjamin Franklin's head. But now, as we watched, he took off flapping toward the stairs to the State Floor.

Here is something I learned that day: When you've got a bunch of people stuck in a hallway, a tiny, harmless bird causes almost as much freak-out as a big, galloping dog.

People jumped, they waved, they ducked—and the more they got excited, the more Humdinger fluttered and flew.

Everybody had a suggestion:

"Try birdseed!"

"A cat!"

"Who's got a net?"

Finally, reinforcements arrived, including a couple of Park Service rangers from outside. Together we ran after Humdinger as he fluttered up the stairs to the

East Room, where he found a perch above a famous portrait of George Washington.

The poor little bird's chest rose and fell like he was exhausted, and Tessa said, "Cammie, what if he has a heart attack?"

Next to me, a kid's voice spoke. "I can get him."

I looked over and saw our friend Dalton. He's seven like Tessa, and his family was staying with us for a few days. He must've heard the excitement and come down from upstairs.

As we watched, one of the rangers placed a ladder by the fireplace below the Washington portrait. Tessa waved to get the ranger's attention. "Let me try! I'm a good climber."

Dalton scoffed. "You get dizzy at the top of the jungle gym!"

"*Do not*," Tessa said.

"*Do, too*," Dalton said.

Oh, no. Not this again. My mom and Dalton's dad went to college together. Now Dalton's dad is some kind of money expert who helps out the government sometimes. Anyway, our two families have been friends forever, and Dalton and Tessa always compete. But we didn't have time for it now. And honestly? Dalton's a lot less of a klutz than my sister.

"Tessa," I said, "stay right where you are. Dalton, go on. Give it a try."

Up the ladder he went, and a couple of minutes later, Humdinger had hopped onto his finger. As Dalton climbed down, everyone in the East Room—except Tessa—clapped and cheered.

Upstairs in the Family Kitchen, Dalton put Humdinger safely back in his cage, closed the cage door and latched it. Then Granny got three pink twisty ties from a drawer and wrapped them around the bars of the cage door.

"I always add twisties," she said, "for extra security."

Mr. Bryant—he's our friend and Granny's special friend—was in the kitchen with us. He had been studying the birdcage, and now he shook his head. "I don't see how the little fellow escaped."

"Plus," I said, "how did he get all the way down to the ground floor?"

"Don't look at me!" Dalton said.

"Of course not," Granny said. "We owe you a debt of gratitude."

Dalton looked confused.

Tessa said, "*Duh*, Dalton—she's just using a lot of words to say 'thank you.'"

"Oh," said Dalton. "I knew that. *Duh*."

"All right, everyone, time to wash up," Granny said.

Dalton and his family were staying in a suite on the third floor. Tessa and I share a bedroom on the second floor over the North Portico—that's the White House front door. I was soaping my hands in our bathroom when I heard an earsplitting scream.

What now?

I sighed, turned off the water, dried my hands and walked back into the bedroom. Tessa was standing in front of her laundry hamper with her mouth open. The hamper was empty, and dirty clothes were scattered all over the floor.

"*My piggy bank,*" Tessa said breathlessly. "*It's gone!*"

CHAPTER THREE

TESSA'S piggy bank is the old-fashioned pottery kind. It doesn't have a stopper, so the idea is that when it's full, you have to break it. With Tessa, this will never be a problem. She is terrible at saving. Anyway, the bank came from Mexico, and it's pink, and it used to have red and white roses on it—but now they're kind of flaking off.

If you're wondering why she was staring at the laundry hamper, it's because that's where she hides her piggy bank.

"How much money was in it?" I asked. "Like ninety-eight cents?"

Tessa sniffed. "More than that."

Along with Tessa's clothes on the floor were crayons and paper from some project she'd been doing yesterday. Mrs. Hedges, the maid who cleans our room, was going to have a fit if we didn't get it all picked up.

I looked at my sister and got a surprise: Her face was scrunched like she wanted to cry! This was weird. My sister is a drama queen, but not a crybaby.

"Are you okay?" I asked. "I mean, it's gotta be somewhere. You probably just stuck it in a drawer or something."

Tessa wiped her eyes, shook her head and took a breath. "Okay. You're right. It's not like there could be some piggy bank thief running around."

There are three dining rooms in the residence part of the White House. The two on the State Floor are for fancy company, like queens and quarterbacks. The one on the second floor, where we were eating that day, is mostly for our family and friends.

Granny and Mr. Bryant were already there with Hooligan when Tessa and I walked in. It turned out Mr. Ng was taking his lunch break, and Granny had agreed that Hooligan could stay with us in the dining room.

"Sit down, you two," Granny told Tessa and me. This caused Hooligan to sit down, too...under the table. "Your mom—" Granny started to say.

I finished the sentence. "—is too busy running the country to eat with us."

Tessa crossed her arms over her chest. "Well, *that's* unusual."

Granny didn't comment, just dropped into the chair Mr. Bryant held out for her. Then Mr. Bryant took a seat where our dad would usually be. Most Saturdays Dad's here with us, but this weekend he'd stayed in California. That's where he has a job building airplanes.

Over the next few minutes, six more people came in. They were Dalton; his mom and dad; his brother,

Zach; and my aunt Jen and her son, Nate. Like Granny, Aunt Jen and Nate live here with us in the White House.

Zach sat next to me. He's twelve, two years older than I am. He's nice and everything, but kind of nerdy.

Lunch was chicken salad sandwiches with macaroni salad and cut-up celery, carrots and peppers. Everyone else in America eats potato chips with their sandwiches, but Aunt Jen has my whole family on an eat-healthy kick. Sometimes a person is lucky to get a cookie around here.

Meanwhile, Dalton—the lucky pup—is a total candy fiend, and his parents don't even care.

Mr. Patel, one of the butlers, served the lunch, while everybody talked about what they'd done that morning. Dalton and Zach's dad, Dr. Maynard, said he'd been in a meeting, and then had been practicing for the ceremony that was happening in the Rose Garden the next afternoon.

"What ceremony?" Tessa asked.

Dalton answered. "It's the whole reason we're even visiting, Tessa! Dad's giving some guy from some museum a medal. The guy was really brave or something, right?"

Mrs. Maynard pressed her lips together to keep from laughing. "Not exactly," she said. "And mind your manners, Dalton. The medal is the first national award for a contribution to numismatics."

Tessa asked, "What's numis-whatever-you-said?"

Zach made a face. "Now we'll be here all afternoon."

"Very funny, son," said Dr. Maynard. "It's pronounced 'noo-miz-MAT-ics,' Tessa, and it's the study of money."

Tessa had been about to take a bite, but now she stopped. "You mean money like coins?"

"Coins, beads, seashells—whatever people use for economic transactions," Dr. Maynard said. "It's a fascinating subject. At least, I think so."

Tessa put down her sandwich. "Well, *that's* interesting. So do you know...uh...a lot of stuff about coins?"

"I do, actually," said Dr. Maynard. "And it's nice to hear some enthusiasm on the subject"—he looked at Dalton and Zach—"for a change."

Zach said, "I like money fine."

Dalton nodded. "But coins are boring."

Dr. Maynard sighed. "Anyway, Tessa, you may not realize that the National Museum of American History has the biggest collection of coins and money anywhere. If you're really interested, we might be able to arrange a tour. Only, the family and I have to leave Monday, so there's not much time."

Granny said, "I'm sure Cammie and Nate would like to see the coins, too."

And next thing you know, the grown-ups were checking calendars and Dr. Maynard was texting his friend at the museum. Before I could even finish my sandwich, the whole thing was arranged. We were going to look at the coin collection that very same night.

"This is turning out to be quite an educational Saturday for you children," Mr. Bryant said. "Archaeology this afternoon, the museum tonight."

"At least the archaeology part'll be fun," Dalton said. "I want to dig up a mummy!"

"The archeologist—his name's Professor Mudd—is looking for historic artifacts from the nineteenth century, not mummies, Dalton," said my cousin Nate, who is ten like me and thinks he knows everything.

"Also, mummies are in Egypt, Dalton—*duh*," said Tessa.

"I knew that—*duh*," said Dalton.

"Bet you didn't," said Tessa.

"Bet I did," said Dalton.

"Bet you—"

"*Awh-roohr!*" Hooligan howled, which for once was a welcome interruption.

Tessa reached down to pet him, then made a face. "*Ewwwww*—puppy, what's the matter with your mouth? It's bloody!"

I took a look and saw colored blotches on Hooligan's tongue and the fur around his mouth. "I don't think it's blood," I said, "I mean, unless some of Hooligan's blood is green."

Mrs. Maynard laid her fork down and frowned. "*Dalton?*"

Dalton didn't look at his mom. He looked at Granny and said, "May I be excused, please?"

"Yes, you may, young man," Granny said, "but before you go, could you hold out your hands?"

Reluctantly, Dalton did, and we all saw the right one was colored the same as Hooligan's mouth, red and green.

Mr. Bryant chuckled. "Kind of gives new meaning to the phrase 'caught red-handed,' doesn't it?"

Granny said, "Jelly beans?"

Zach said, "Man, she's good."

Mrs. Maynard looked embarrassed. "Dalton did bring a few bags of jelly beans with him this trip."

"A few?" Zach said.

"Christmas colors were on sale," Dr. Maynard explained.

Dalton grinned. "I've got so many I'm even a little sick of 'em. But Hooligan thinks they're delicious!"

Hooligan thumped his tail in agreement.

Then Granny explained that jelly beans aren't healthy food for dogs. And Aunt Jen pointed out they're not healthy for people, either. And Mrs. Maynard, looking embarrassed, promised that if Hooligan got sick, Dalton would pay the vet bill out of his own allowance.

Finally, Dalton said he was sorry like ten times, and that he hoped he could still help with the dig out on the South Lawn.

The answer to that was yes—I think because his parents thought Dalton would get in less trouble outside than in.

CHAPTER FOUR

AFTER lunch, Mr. Bryant took all of us kids—Tessa, me, Nate, Dalton and Zach—out to the South Lawn through the Diplomatic Reception Room. That winter in Washington had been rainy and cold, but now it was the start of spring, and for once a sunny day. We passed under the Dip Room awning, then walked past the Rose Garden and down toward the swimming pool.

Even though we were basically in our own back-yard, we were protected by Secret Service people. Malik, Jeremy and Charlotte and the other officers and agents do their best to stay out of our way, though, as much as they can. That's because my parents want us to feel like normal kids.

Soon we could see the big white canopy Professor Mudd and his crew had put up yesterday. The space underneath was set up like an office, with tables, chairs and storage cupboards. As we got closer, we saw that an area of lawn had been marked off with wooden stakes and orange plastic tape.

A skinny man with a brown beard came out to meet us. Mr. Bryant had already met him, and introduced us. His name was Mike, and he was one of the college students working on the dig.

"Welcome to the offices of Dig, Inc., White House branch," he said, grinning. "We're glad to see you. We can always use new shovelbums."

"Shovelbums?" I repeated.

"You know, dig? Shovel?" Mike said. "A shovelbum is anyone who helps us out."

Besides Mike, there were five people under the canopy in the dig's "office." Seated at a desk was a big man with bushy gray eyebrows and the kind of helmet people wear in TV shows about safaris. Standing behind him were two women and two men. All of them were studying a computer screen and talking, and you could see they were excited.

The man with the eyebrows shook his head. "You kids realize I don't trust this new technology any farther than I can throw it. I bet there's a bug in the detector, or maybe the software."

"I don't think so, Professor. I checked it out myself," said one of the women. "All indications are that we've found gold."

Gold?

No wonder they were excited!

And now so were we. "Mike, can we go look at the screen, too?" Nate asked.

"Sure, why not?" Mike said. "Come on over, and I'll introduce you."

The man in the helmet turned out to be Professor Mudd, and the others were students like Mike—Wen Fei, Stephanie, Roy and Daryl.

The computer display they were looking at had multicolored specks and blobs on a background marked off in squares. One of the blobs stood out brighter than the rest, a sunlike yellow dot near the top right corner.

"Just what is it we're looking at here, if you don't mind my asking?" said Mr. Bryant.

Professor Mudd snorted. "Prior to the California Gold Rush in 1849, there was very little gold in the United States. The archeological remains we're looking for date from long before that, 1814 through 1817. It's Wen Fei here who insisted on trying out a new gadget. If you ask me, the gadget's gone haywire."

"What kind of new gadget?" Nate asked.

"Fancy metal detector," Mike explained. "Excavating a site—digging, in other words—is expensive and takes a lot of time. So before we start, we do a survey to decide where we should focus. Yesterday Wen Fei did part of the survey using a new neutron-scatter device that gives a readout on the properties of the metal it finds." He pointed at the computer screen. "The different colored markings are different types of metal, see? And Wen Fei and Stephanie are convinced that yellow one shows gold below the surface at the northeast corner of the dig site—about halfway between here and the Rose Garden."

"How much gold?" Zach asked. "Like a treasure chest?"

Stephanie laughed. "Not hardly. The technology's very sensitive. What we found looked more like about an ounce. Could be a coin, maybe."

All during the last few minutes, Tessa had been shifting her weight from foot to foot, and now she tugged my sleeve. "Cammie? I don't feel so good."

"What is it?" I asked.

She put her hand on her tummy and made a face.

"I can walk back with you, young lady," Mr. Bryant said. "Are the rest of you children all right?"

"We're going to put them right to work, sir," Mike said. "In fact, Daryl's got a spot for them all picked out."

CHAPTER FIVE

AFTER Tessa and Mr. Bryant left, Daryl took me, Nate, Dalton and Zach over to a big metal cupboard with tools inside. Each of us got a trowel, a mesh strainer and a pair of gloves. Then we followed Daryl to a shallow trench on the side of the canopy closest to the swimming pool, and he showed us what to do: cut into the dirt with the trowel, break up any clumps, then shake the dirt through the strainer like flour through a sifter.

"What are we looking for, exactly?" I asked.

Daryl answered my question with a question. "You guys know British soldiers burned down the White House in August of 1814, right?"

"That was during the administration of James Madison," Nate said. "The fire destroyed everything but the outer walls, and rebuilding took three years."

Zach looked worried. "Is there going to be a quiz?"

Daryl laughed. "No quiz. I'm just giving you some background so you know what you're looking for. See, a fire makes a heck of a mess, and in those days there weren't any dump trucks for hauling trash away to the landfill. Now you mention it, there weren't any land-fills. So what they did was dump the trash right out here—burnt timber and bricks, doors, broken windows, china, pretty much whatever you can think of that was destroyed in the fire."

"Yuck—you mean we're digging for burned-up trash?" Dalton said.

Daryl grinned. "Now that it's been underground so long, you can't call it trash, exactly. Come right down to it, you're looking for anything that isn't dirt. Could be a nail, a piece of glass, maybe even a piece of teacup."

After that, Daryl asked if we had questions, and none of us did, so he left us to dig on our own. It was fun, like being a little kid in a sandbox. About an hour went by and nobody found anything. I was starting to get bored when, finally, something showed up in my strainer. It was hard, lighter than a rock and sort of leaf-shaped, but so covered with dirt and grime I couldn't tell if it was important.

I showed Nate, who wasn't impressed, but Zach said, "Maybe it's a relic, Cammie. You'd better mark where you found it and show it to Professor Mudd."

Daryl and Mike were just on the other side of the canopy, and I held out my find for them to see.

"Do you think it's important?" I asked.

"Sure. Could be," Mike said. "Stephanie will clean it up and analyze it."

"How long will that take?" I asked.

"Tomorrow sometime," Daryl said. "Just right now,

I'm not sure where either she or Wen Fei has got to. I think they're pretty annoyed that Professor Mudd doesn't believe their new metal detector's working right."

Mike came back to the trench with me and noted the exact depth and location where I had found whatever-it-was. Then he asked, "How are the rest of you getting along?"

"I'm bored," Dalton said.

Mike laughed. "Yeah, I hear you. But hey, unlike us, you guys are volunteers. Feel free to take a break."

"We had an idea...if it's okay." Nate set down his trowel and pointed. "Northeast is over there, right? Could we go have a look?"

Mike understood right away. "For the gold, you mean? Sure, but you realize whatever's over there's underground, right? And since it's part of the dig site, you can't disturb the surface without permission from Professor Mudd."

"We just want to see the spot," Nate said. "Then maybe later, if it's okay, we can dig for buried treasure!"

Mike gave his okay, and we took off.

If you have a bad sense of direction, the White House is a good place to live. All you have to do is remember the north and south porticoes and the east and west wings, and you can't really get confused. Since the dig site was marked out on the lawn with tape and stakes, I expected we'd find the northeast corner without that much trouble.

The way it turned out, though, it was totally no trouble.

That's because someone had been there before us. And pretty much right where the computer screen said the gold was supposed to be, there was only a hole in the ground!

CHAPTER SIX

THE hole, about a foot wide and six inches deep, made a brown blotch in the green grass. Nate said, "We'd better tell Professor Mudd right away," and we were going to do just that when we heard a horrible *screech-yeowwwww* that could only mean one thing: cat in crisis!

I looked toward the sound, and there it was—a black-and-white furball streaking across the grass.

Maybe "streak" is the wrong word.

For sure, the cat was moving as fast as it possibly could, but it was so fat that its motion was more like waddling in a hurry.

A few seconds behind it, singing *"Arrh-arrh-arrh"* in a squeaky soprano and moving a whole lot faster, came a beagle I recognized right away.

"Pickles—*no!*" I shouted, and took off sprinting to intercept him. "You leave that poor kitty alone!"

Pickles belongs to Ms. Ann Major, who is a deputy assistant associate in my mom's press office. He and

Hooligan went to obedience school together, and now they have playdates sometimes.

I was out of breath when I caught up to Pickles by a hedge halfway to the Rose Garden. The hedge must be where the cat had its hideout.

"Pickles, *come*," I said, which caused him to look up and wag his tail before he went back to sniffing under the hedge. So much for obedience school.

Meanwhile, I heard running footsteps behind me and turned around. There was Ms. Major, also out of breath. And right behind her were Nate, Zach and Dalton.

"Oh, that darned cat!" Ms. Major said, which didn't seem exactly fair. I mean, the cat was just trying to survive. It was Pickles who was acting all bloodthirsty.

But I like Ms. Major, and she helped Nate, Tessa and me solve a mystery once, so what I said was "I never saw that cat before."

"It's a stray, and it's been hanging around for a few weeks," Ms. Major said. "I think somebody's feeding it, because it used to be pathetic and scrawny, but now it's got a belly like a bowling ball."

"Tessa's been bugging Granny for a cat," I said. "If she finds out about this one, she'll never shut up."

"Oh, I think she knows already," Ms. Major said. "I saw her and Hooligan both out here yesterday afternoon."

By then, I guess, the cat had gotten away, because Pickles trotted over to us and sat down like an obedience school star student. Ms. Major sighed, then scratched him behind the ears. "You don't fool me for one minute, you know."

"How come you have to work on a Saturday, Ms. Major?" Nate asked.

"I work most Saturdays, it seems like," she said. "Today I have to do some prep for that ceremony coming up tomorrow. It'll amount to ten seconds on TV if we're lucky, but it still takes some work. I don't generally bring the pooch in, but he's got a therapy appointment across town."

"Dog therapy?" I said.

Ms. Major nodded and tapped her head. "The mental kind. He's terrified of thunder, poor thing—goes absolutely crazy in a storm. The therapist is supposed to help him take control of his fear."

Nate said, "Really? Is it working?"

Ms. Major shrugged. "Who knows? There hasn't been a storm since he started."

Since Dalton and Zach hadn't met Ms. Major, I introduced them. Then Ms. Major said, "It's your dad giving the medal at the ceremony tomorrow, isn't it? I hope I get to meet him afterward. I have questions about some old coins of mine...if he doesn't mind, that is."

"He won't mind," Zach said. "He'd talk about coins all day if he could."

I wanted to tell Ms. Major about the dig and the gold and the mysterious hole in the ground, but she had already scooped up Pickles. "I'd better get back to work," she said. "We don't want anything to go wrong tomorrow."

When Ms. Major was gone, we four kids headed back to the dig office. We wanted to tell Professor Mudd about the hole we'd found.

The way it turned out, though, we weren't the ones to break the news. As we approached, we saw Mike talking to him. "Hold on to your helmet, sir," Mike said. "I've just had a look around the site, and it's like Swiss cheese out there—seven unauthorized holes at least! What do you think? Could Wen Fei and Stephanie be right about the gold? Could someone be digging for buried treasure?"

CHAPTER SEVEN

INSTEAD of answering Mike's questions, Professor Mudd sat at his desk and scowled. Was he mad? Or just thinking? With his bushy eyebrows, it was hard to tell the difference. Either way, I felt intimidated, and I guess Zach, Nate and Dalton did, too, because several seconds passed with us all standing around in silence. Finally, Professor Mudd looked straight at me. "Yes, Cameron?"

I gulped and said in a small voice, "We found a hole, too."

Professor Mudd snorted, threw up his hands and called, "Roy? Bring the maps and come with Mike and me. We'll have to plot the locations of these dratted holes. Buried treasure—ha! That's the *last* thing I need. Oh—and Daryl? Could you help our young volunteers clean up, please? We'll see you kids back tomorrow, I trust? I realize it's Sunday."

"Yes, sir," I said. "If it's okay, I mean."

"Why wouldn't it be okay?" the professor said. Then he grabbed a clipboard and left.

After that, Daryl went with us to the trench where we had been digging so we could retrieve our tools, clean them up and put them away. All this time I hadn't seen Stephanie or Wen Fei anywhere. Had they left because they were mad the professor didn't believe that their new gadget had found gold? But now it looked like somebody else believed it. Otherwise, what were all these holes doing out here?

"I don't get it," I said a few minutes later. Nate, Dalton, Zach and I were walking back toward the White House with Jeremy, who had come over from his station at the west fence to accompany us. "Why isn't Professor Mudd excited about the idea there might be gold out there?"

"That's just how professors are," Zach said. "I mean, our dad's one, so that's how I know. Probably, Professor Mudd's already sure what he's going to find at that dig site. If he finds something different, like gold, then that means he was wrong."

I nodded. "I get it. If there's one thing grown-ups hate, it's being wrong."

Zach nodded. "Professors hate it most of all."

This gave me an idea. "Hey, Nate—maybe you should be a professor when you grow up. I mean, you already think you know everything."

Nate didn't argue or act insulted. He just nodded and said, "You're right."

By then we were back at the door to the White House, the South Entrance under the Dip Room awning. Malik, my second-favorite Secret Service officer, was stationed outside. We said hi to him and bye to Jeremy, then went inside.

On the stairs to the second floor, Nate asked, "Cammie, are you thinking what I'm thinking?"

I grinned because I was. "You mean how the holes and the missing gold are almost like a mystery?"

Nate looked at his watch. "And it's not that late. How about if we make a list?"

Zach and Dalton didn't know what we were talking about, so Nate explained. The first time we solved a mystery, Granny gave us tips, and one thing she told us to do was to start by writing a list of everything we knew.

"Granny is the only person in our family with actual crime-fighting experience," I added. "A long time ago, before she was a lawyer and a judge, she used to be a police officer."

At the second-floor landing, we agreed to meet in a few minutes in the West Sitting Hall. In the whole White House, it's got the most comfortable sofa, so it's my favorite spot for thinking.

First, though, I wanted to check on my sick sister.

I thought I'd find her in her pajamas in bed, or—yuck—in the bathroom.

But when I went into our room, I got a big surprise.

My sister was dressed, sitting on the floor and folding clothes.

Okay, so that was strange, but it wasn't the surprise. The surprise was how the rest of our room looked pretty much like Kansas after the cyclone!

CHAPTER EIGHT

FOR a minute, I stood in the doorway and surveyed the damage. Not only were most of Tessa's clothes on the floor, but every dresser drawer was open, her bedding was flung everywhere and two chairs had been tipped over. There were still crayons and paper on the floor by the love seat, too.

I had a scary thought. What if Tessa had a fever and it had gone to her brain?

I haven't been around a lot of crazy people, but from movies I get the idea that you're supposed to stay calm so you don't upset them.

So, very quietly, I said, "Uh...Tessa? Could you tell me what you're doing?"

Tessa didn't look up. "Sure, Cammie. I'm putting my clothes away."

So far, so good.

"Uh, okay. But did something happen?" Then I had another idea. "Wait, was it Hooligan?"

Tessa shook her head. "For once, you can't blame

Hooligan. How 'bout if I said I had an irresistible urge to tidy up for Mrs. Hedges? Would you believe that?"

I crossed my arms over my chest. "No."

Tessa sighed and folded another T-shirt. "Didn't think so," she said. "So okay, the truth is I was looking for my piggy bank, but I can't find it anywhere! And now I'm pretty sure for real it must be stolen."

"How much money was in it?" I asked.

"Two dollars and twelve cents," Tessa said. "Plus a little more."

"I don't think that's enough for anyone to steal it," I said.

"Do you think someone could've really wanted the bank part?" Tessa asked. "Do you think it could be, like, an antique?"

"No way," I said. "I mean, no offense, but with the paint flaking off, it looked like a piggy bank with pimples."

Tessa dropped what she'd been folding. "You take that back!"

I shrugged. "Fine. But only because I have to meet Zach, Nate and Dalton. We might have a new mystery to solve." Tessa had been there when we found out about the gold, but I had to explain about the holes. "Do you feel better?" I asked. "Do you want to help us?"

Tessa shook her head. "I've got my own mystery to solve: the case of the piggy bank thief."

CHAPTER NINE

NATE, Zach and Dalton were waiting for me in the West Sitting Hall. "Is Tessa any better?" Nate wanted to know.

It was too much to explain about the piggy bank.

"She looks better," I said, "but she isn't up for solving a mystery yet."

"What is it we're doing, again?" Dalton asked.

I had gotten my notebook from my desk, and I held it up for him to see. "I write," I explained, "and everybody else talks."

Zach, Dalton and Nate totally took that last part seriously. I mean, I had barely sat down before they all started yakking at once. I wrote as fast as I could to keep up:

- *New gadget shows gold buried under northwest corner of dig site.*
- *Gold was found Friday afternoon by Wen Fei (student) when she surveyed the site.*

- *Saturday afternoon when Zach, Nate, Cammie, Dalton went to look, no gold, only hole.*
- *Mike found at least seven holes around dig site.*
- *Professor Mudd says gadget is probably wrong, probably no gold.*
- *Wen Fei and Stephanie mad because Professor Mudd doesn't believe in gold.*

"Can we put questions on the list?" Zach said.

"Sure," I said.

"Okay, I want to ask how we know if any gold is really missing," Zach said.

I wrote that down, then added two more questions:

- *Who dug the holes?*
- *Why did they dig the holes?*
- *Was it because they expected to find gold?*

So much writing made my fingers tired. Now I stopped for a second and shook them out.

Nate said, "We should mention the fat, waddling cat."

Zach said, "Why? That doesn't have anything to do with the missing gold."

"Granny says to write down anything strange, even if we don't see how it's related," I explained. "And the cat was out there where the gold was supposed to be."

Zach grinned. "Plus, cats dig, too, you know? Like when they—"

"Ewww!" I made a face. "I am not writing *that* part down."

What I did write was:

- *Fat, waddling cat hangs out in hedge between dig site and Rose Garden.*

"If we're going to write that, then we should go ahead and put in the other strange thing that happened today—Humdinger," Nate said. "You know, how he got out and went downstairs."

"Wait...what?" Dalton said. "No! I mean, that doesn't have anything to do with the missing gold. It's not like it was even outside."

I shrugged. "It does seem crazy. But Granny says we should pay attention to coincidences."

Dalton frowned, and I wrote:

- *Humdinger escaped from cage (how?), flew downstairs (how?) and practically caused riot among million White House visitors.*

"Now what do we do?" Zach asked.

"We study the list and see if anything looks extra weird," Nate said.

"Like the timing. See?" I said. "Wen Fei did her survey yesterday afternoon, and there was no hole out there then. So the hole was dug and the gold disappeared sometime after that but before we were out there today."

Nate nodded. "Right. So whoever dug up the gold must have done it overnight or earlier today."

"That's good," Zach said. "It eliminates about ninety-nine-point-nine percent of the population. After all, the White House has a big fence around it and it's guarded. The only people out there those times are people allowed to be out there."

I said, "In other words, us, the staff, the Secret Service, the marines, the Park Service people and the people who work in the West Wing, like Ms. Major. That's still a lot."

"There's something else, though," Nate said. "The thief has to be somebody who knew there was gold in the first place."

"And that's almost nobody," Zach said. "I mean, the only people who knew about the gold are Wen Fei and Stephanie, right?"

"But what about the other students?" I asked. "And Professor Mudd?"

Zach shrugged. "But none of them believes it about the gold."

"And there's something else I thought of," Nate said. "What happened to Wen Fei and Stephanie today? After the argument with Professor Mudd, they disappeared."

"They were mad," I said. "He wasn't very nice to them."

"That's one explanation," Nate said. "But here's another one: Maybe they were making their getaway with the gold! I don't know about you guys, but right now I'd say Wen Fei and Stephanie are our prime suspects."

CHAPTER TEN

MY cousin Nate is some kind of piano genius, and now he had to go practice. With him gone, detecting was officially on hold.

And I had nothing to do till dinner.

Uh-oh.

Was it possible I would have to take extreme measures?

Like doing my homework for Monday even though it wasn't Sunday night yet?

Back in our bedroom, Tessa had tidied up, except for the crayons and drawing paper. Cleaning must have tired her out, because she was lying on her bed, staring at the ceiling. I told her we had figured out that Wen Fei and Stephanie might be suspects, partly because they were the only ones who really believed there was gold at the dig site at all.

Tessa didn't say anything. I guessed she was still upset. "Do you want me to help you look for your piggy bank?" I asked.

Tessa still didn't say anything, but I opened my notebook. Looking for an old piggy bank was better than doing homework. "When did you have it last?" I asked.

Tessa sighed and sat up. "It won't help, Cammie. But okay. It was yesterday before dinner. I remember because I...uh...made a deposit."

I wrote that down. "And then what did you do with it?"

"Put it away in the laundry hamper."

"Okay," I said. "And when did you realize it was missing?"

"You know already." Tessa was getting aggravated, which wasn't very fair considering I was being so nice. "It was today right before lunch. I opened the hamper to put my leotard from ballet in. I thought the piggy bank was on top but I didn't see it, so I emptied everything out and still didn't see it."

"That's when you screamed," I said.

Tessa nodded. "I don't see how anybody could have stolen it—that's the weird part. I mean, my laundry hamper is the best hiding place ever."

I probably shouldn't have laughed, but I couldn't help it. "I have news for you, Tessa. You are so proud of that hiding place, you've told everybody. Half the White House knows where you keep your piggy bank."

Tessa pouted. "No, I didn't, and no, they don't."

"Yes, they do, too," I said, "and I can prove it. Come on."

CHAPTER ELEVEN

TESSA moaned but finally got up and followed me out our bedroom door and into the Center Hall. There we found Mrs. Hedges, the grumpiest maid in the White House. Hands on hips, head tilted, she was staring at a valuable and historic painting of a ship.

Instead of "Hello," Mrs. Hedges said, "Does that look straight to you?"

Tessa and I are used to Mrs. Hedges. We went and stood next to her and stared at the painting.

"I think it's tilted to the left," I said, but Tessa said, "No, right."

Mrs. Hedges nodded. "*Exactly.* It's crooked. And who'll get the blame for that? Me." She shook her head. "My job's not easy, girls. You know that?"

"We do, Mrs. Hedges," I said.

"All right, then. What is it you want?"

"Could you answer a question?" I asked.

Mrs. Hedges looked around for an armchair, then

dropped into it and made herself comfortable. "I hope it's not a hard one."

"It's not," I said. "Here goes: Where does Tessa keep her piggy bank?"

Mrs. Hedges laughed. "Tessa keeps her piggy bank in her laundry hamper. Everyone knows that."

It's almost as useless to argue with Mrs. Hedges as it is to argue with Granny. But Tessa tried. "Everyone does not! You do because you clean our room!"

Mrs. Hedges shook her head. "Beg to differ with you there. I don't have time for laundry when I'm cleaning. Why, yesterday it took five minutes just to scrub your dirty sink."

Tessa turned pink and hung her head. "Sorry, Mrs. Hedges."

"I know about your hiding place," Mrs. Hedges went on, "because you told me. Same as you told Malik, and Mr. Bryant, and Mr. Ng, and Charlotte, and Mr. Ross, and—"

"Okay, okay," Tessa said. "I guess I did happen to mention it to a few very trustworthy people."

"It wouldn't matter that much, Tessa," I said, "except now there're no suspects we can eliminate. Almost anybody in the White House could have taken your piggy bank. What I can't figure out is—why?"

CHAPTER TWELVE

HAVE you ever felt like an idea was knocking on your skull, but your brain wouldn't let it in? That was the feeling I had that afternoon. It had something to do with a connection between the two mysteries, the one about the piggy bank and the one about the gold—but what was it?

I didn't have time to consider the question, though. Granny was making an early dinner for Nate, Tessa and me. Later Aunt Jen and Charlotte—she's my favorite Secret Service agent—would take us to the museum. Zach and Dalton were having dinner with their parents at a restaurant, then meeting us.

When Tessa and I got to the family kitchen, Nate was already at the table, and Hooligan was under it. Granny had made hamburgers, and Mr. Bryant served our plates. Then he sat down in a spare chair by the stove, and Granny leaned back against the counter. She was wearing an apron for cooking, but under it was a shiny red-and-white dress I'd never seen before.

"Aren't you eating anything?" I asked Mr. Bryant.

"Your grandmother and I have dinner plans later," he said, "but those burgers do smell good."

Tessa held her plate out and smiled. "You can have a bite of my hamburger if you want."

I could see Mr. Bryant was thinking about it, but Granny spoke up. "Don't you dare, Willis! You're slow enough on the tennis court."

Mr. Bryant sighed and looked from Tessa to me to Nate. "You see what I put up with?"

Tessa nodded sympathetically. "I know. She acts like that with us, too, sometimes. But deep down she's nice."

"Did you play tennis this afternoon, Granny? Who won?" Nate asked between bites.

"I did, as usual," Granny said.

Mr. Bryant raised his eyebrows. " 'As usual'? That's not the outcome I remember yesterday."

Granny's mouth was set in a straight line, but there were smile crinkles around her eyes. "What are you talking about? Personally, I don't remember that far back. Must be my advanced age."

"You can ask me about yesterday," said Tessa, " 'cause my advanced age is seven. And it was me who watched Hooligan so you could play, remember? Afterward, Mr. Bryant said he beat Granny big-time."

Hearing his name, Hooligan shifted in his sleep. Usually, he would have been begging for burgers, but not today. Maybe he was still full of jelly beans?

Meanwhile, Nate had set his fork down. "Wait a

sec. Tessa, you were outside with Hooligan yesterday afternoon?"

Tessa's jaw froze midchew.

"That's right," I said. "I totally forgot, but Ms. Major said she saw you, and Hooligan was sniffing in the bushes where the stray cat lives."

"Stray cat?" Granny said.

Oops. I hadn't meant to bring that up. Granny didn't want to listen to any more whining from Tessa on the cat subject.

But now I had to explain, so I did, and the second I stopped talking, Granny raised a warning hand. "Don't you even start, Tessa. I know how much you want a cat, but I don't see how that's ever going to work with this canine of yours."

"But Hooligan *loves* kitties!" Tessa nudged him with her toe. "Don't you, puppy?"

Nathan laughed. "Loves to munch them, you mean. Right, buddy?"

Hooligan opened his eyes and said, *"Woof,"* which did not exactly answer the question. Our dog hasn't been around cats much. Was Tessa right, or was Nate?

"You're not one bit funny, Nathan," Tessa said. "And anyway, I don't want some old grown-up cat. I want a cute, furry little kitten."

Nate rubbed his belly. "Mmmmm...even more delicious!"

Tessa whined, "Grannyyyy! Make him stop!"

Granny gave Nate a look; he shrugged and changed the subject. "Tessa, if you were out by the dig yesterday, you might be an important witness. Did you see Wen Fei and Stephanie? Did you see anybody digging holes?"

Tessa didn't answer right away. Instead, she took a bite of her hamburger, chewed, swallowed and dabbed her mouth politely. Finally, she asked who Wen Fei and Stephanie were, and when Nate reminded her, she said, "Oh. Uh...and where did you say the dig is, again?"

I couldn't believe my sister. "We were there this afternoon!"

"Oh, right," she said. "Uh...nope, didn't see a thing."

I looked at Tessa. "Are you sure you feel okay? Because you're acting kind of crazy."

"Well, maybe I don't want to be interrogated!" she snapped.

Nate and I looked at each other. What the heck?

Then Mr. Bryant said, "Sounds like there might be some more detecting going on. Do I have that right?"

Nate explained about the maybe gold that was maybe missing.

"A buried piece of gold?" Granny said. "Could it be a coin, do you think? If so, then you're going to the right place tonight to do some more detecting."

CHAPTER THIRTEEN

THE National Museum of American History, part of the Smithsonian Institution, is wide and white, with a fountain on one side and a statue that looks like silver ribbon on the other. It's on the National Mall in Washington, DC—pretty near my house. Inside is cool stuff like race cars and steam engines, five-hundred-year-old violins, mannequins wearing beautiful First Lady dresses and the ruby slippers from *The Wizard of Oz*.

Usually there would be lots of people inside, too, but Dr. Maynard had arranged for us to visit when the museum was closed. That's why when Nate, Tessa, Aunt Jen, Charlotte and I walked through the heavy glass doors, only two guards and a man in a suit and tie met us. The man was Dr. Maynard's friend, a curator named Mr. August—the same guy who would be getting a medal at the ceremony the next day.

After the usual handshakes and "how are yous?" Mr. August took all of us up in an elevator to a room on the fifth floor, where Zach and Dalton and their parents were waiting for us.

"Welcome to our library," said Mr. August.

The room had blue walls and bookcases, but it was small and not exactly fancy. In fact, with all of us in there, it was kind of a tight squeeze.

"Aren't we going to see an exhibit?" Tessa asked. "Like when we went to see the Hope Diamond?"

Mr. August shook his head. "Our collection is so big we can only display a few things at a time. The rest is kept in the vault. When Dr. Maynard told me you're also working on Professor Mudd's dig, I decided to get out some coins from the same time period—early American history."

There was a table in the middle of the room. The grown-ups sat around it while Charlotte and us kids stood behind them. On top of the table was a black case like a big jewelry box.

"What's in there?" Tessa pointed.

"You'll see," said Mr. August mysteriously. "But first, I want you all to look in your pockets or coin purses, get out any change you might have and put it on the table."

"What if we don't have any?" Tessa asked.

I told Tessa I'd share. A few seconds later, there was a handful of quarters, dimes, nickels and pennies in front of each of us.

"Most collectors get interested in coins when they examine the ones they have on hand every day," Mr. August said.

Dr. Maynard nodded. "That's what happened to me.

When I learned that coins have dates on them to show when they were made, I got the idea it would be neat to have pennies from as many years as possible. I asked my father for the coins from his pocket, and that's how I started collecting."

Dalton shook his head. "Lame, Dad."

"*Dalton?*" said his mom.

But his dad kept his temper. "It's not lame, Dalton. First of all, coins are beautiful. Each one is a tiny work of sculpture."

Dalton did not seem convinced.

"And second," Dr. Maynard went on, "when you collect coins, it makes every day a little more exciting. After all, you can never tell when your pocket change will hold a treasure."

Dalton didn't say anything to that. He just started examining the coins on the table. And so did I. I mean, who can't get behind treasure?

Meanwhile, Mr. August told us that after the United States declared its independence from Great Britain, it needed its own system of money. Coming up with one might sound like no big deal, but actually it's tough. Like if you're going to use coins, you need enough metal to make them. And if you're going to use paper, you need new designs that are super hard to copy. Most of all, you need something everybody can agree on.

"One way to accomplish that last part is to base the new system on something reliable and familiar," Mr. August said. "That's why the first secretary of the treasury, Alexander Hamilton, picked the Spanish silver dollar. Silver dollars had been used in the New World for almost three hundred years by then. Has anybody ever heard of pieces of eight?"

"Like in pirate movies?" Zach said.

"Exactly," said Mr. August. "Spanish dollars were routinely divided into eighths, which are also called bits. So a piece of eight is an eighth of a dollar. If you look at the coins we use today"—Mr. August picked up a handful from the table—"most of them are in units of ten, right? Ten pennies to a dime, ten dimes to a dollar. But there's one holdover from history, from the old pieces of eight. Does anybody know what that is?"

Usually Nate is the star student, so it was a surprise to everyone—even me—when I answered, "The quarter."

"Good, Cameron. How did you figure that out?" Mr. August asked.

"I know Granny sometimes calls a quarter two bits," I admitted, "and you said a bit is the same as a piece of eight. Two eighths is a quarter, so..."

Nate grumped, "I can't believe I didn't figure that out."

Mr. August said, "Excellent!" and I tried to look modest.

"The point," Mr. August said, "is that the coins in your pocket are a direct link to history. And sometimes they're valuable, too. It's fun to take a look in case you have something old or unusual in your pocket. Now, does anybody want to see what's in the box?"

We all did.

Mr. August opened it to reveal...a lot of smaller

boxes, like the kind you keep earrings in. After he put on a pair of gloves like dentists wear, Mr. August took one of the small boxes and opened it. Inside was a shining gold coin about the size of a quarter. Soon we all had gloves on and were examining it with a magnifier called a loupe, which is pronounced the same as "loop."

On the front of the gold coin was the head of a lady. She was wearing some funky kind of hat over her long hair. Above her it said *Liberty*, and below her, *1796*. The back had an eagle, and clouds and stars. It said *United States of America*.

With the magnifier, you could see tiny details and bumps in the gold. While we took turns looking, Dr. Maynard and Mr. August explained that the coin was minted in Philadelphia and called a quarter eagle because it was worth $2.50, one quarter the value of the $10 eagle coin from 1795 that he showed us next. That one had a scrawny-looking eagle on the back.

There were other coins, too, like a silver dollar from Peru and another one from the United States. They all came from the 1790s, and they all had pictures of ladies with long, curly hair.

"So is this dollar still worth a dollar?" Tessa wanted to know. "And the quarter eagle—is it worth two-fifty?"

Dalton laughed. "Duh, Tessa. Old coins are worth a lot more, right? So, like, that one"—he pointed at the quarter eagle—"is probably worth like twenty dollars by now, right?"

Mr. August smiled. "Well, as a matter of fact, that coin is one of the more valuable objects in the collection because there's something unusual about it. Every other U.S. coin minted during this time had stars on the obverse—that's the front. Usually thirteen, to represent the first states. As you can see, this one doesn't."

"So it's, like, worth more than twenty dollars?" Dalton asked.

"A bit more, yes," said Mr. August. "In fact, the last one that sold at auction sold for well over a million dollars."

CHAPTER FOURTEEN

I guess whatever was bothering Tessa's stomach earlier must have been catching, because after that, Dalton said he wasn't feeling so good, either, and we had to leave. Even though I hadn't been that excited about going to the museum, I was disappointed that we couldn't stay longer. It was cool to look at the coins. You couldn't help wondering what they had bought and who else had held them since they were made—more than two hundred years ago.

From now on, I decided, I'd pay more attention to the change in my pocket.

It was nine o'clock when we got back to the White House, and Tessa and I changed into pajamas. We were reading when Mom came in to say good night. She was still wearing her Madam President clothes. This time it was a pale blue dress with no sleeves and a full skirt. She had already taken off her shoes and her earrings.

"Mama!" Tessa held her arms out for a snuggle. "What a beautiful dress!"

Mom kissed Tessa, then looked down at herself and made a face. "Kind of snug at the moment. I probably shouldn't have had dessert. I know—what would you think if I asked the designers to start using elastic waistbands like the ones on my sweatpants?"

Tessa's terrible frown made Mom and me both laugh. Then Mom gave me a kiss and sat down on the edge of Tessa's bed.

"How's running the country going, Mom?" I asked her.

"Pretty smoothly at the moment." Mom knocked on the wooden headboard of my bed for good luck. "There hasn't been a serious crisis since yesterday, when we severed relations with a small, faraway country. And besides church, the only thing on my schedule tomorrow is that medal ceremony in the Rose Garden. What's the latest with you girls?"

"We went to the museum and Dalton got a tummy-ache," Tessa said.

"The way he eats candy all the time, I'm not surprised," Mom said.

"Aunt Jen told us if you eat too much candy you get fat and your teeth fall out," Tessa said. "But Dalton's not fat and he's got plenty of teeth. Also, he got a hundred bags of jelly beans for Christmas."

Mom yawned. "Interesting."

"And he's still got some jelly beans left," Tessa said.

"Unh-hunh," Mom said.

Then I managed to get a word in. "Did you hear about the archeology dig?"

"I know you helped Professor Mudd," Mom said.

"But did you hear about the holes and the missing gold?" I asked.

Tessa started to interrupt with something else about candy, but Mom asked me to tell her about the gold, and I did.

Tessa raised her hand. "I have a comment about that."

Mom sighed. "Go ahead, muffin."

"*I* think Wen Fei and Stephanie did it," Tessa said. "They're the ones who found the gold first. I mean, if there is gold. Which probably there isn't, like Professor Mudd believes, anyway."

Mom stood up. "I can see that this case is especially mysterious. In fact"—she yawned—"it's so mysterious I don't even know what you're talking about."

"That's okay, Mama," Tessa said. "We've got it under control. You just worry about running the country."

Mom wiped pretend sweat from her forehead. "Phew. Now, good night, muffins. I'll see you for church in the morning."

CHAPTER FIFTEEN

GRANNY thinks it's some kind of big privilege that she lets us sleep in till eight o'clock on Sunday. The way she says it, chickens never sleep in at all, and when she was little she had to get up at five every day to gather the eggs.

Mom says Granny is full of prunes, because Granny lived in downtown Los Angeles when she was little and probably never saw a live chicken till she was twenty-one.

Anyway, that Sunday, we didn't even make it till eight o'clock. A knock on the door woke me when it was still dark. What the heck?

I rolled over and saw that the clock said 7:15.

This was so totally unfair.

"It's Nate," a voice called, "and Zach and Dalton, too. We're going detecting. Do you want to come?"

I got up, put on my bathrobe and opened the door. Zach and Nate were dressed, grinning and wide awake. Dalton was dressed, too, but otherwise he looked more the way I felt—grumpy and sleepy.

"I woke up early thinking about all that money," Nate said, "so I knocked on Zach's door, and he was awake, too."

"What money?"

"Oh, for gosh sakes, Cammie—keep up!" Nate said. "Stephanie said the gold out on the dig site might be a coin. And if it is—what if it's worth a million dollars like the quarter eagle we saw yesterday?"

"We're going out to the dig to look around," Zach said.

Have I mentioned it was practically dark outside?

"You guys," I said, "even if we find something, it's not like we're gonna get to keep it. It's on the White House grounds, so it's government property."

Zach admitted I could be right. "But I bet there'll be, like, a big reward anyway. Are you guys coming or not?"

I said, "Five minutes," and closed the door. No way was I letting Nate, Zach and Dalton go without me.

Tessa was hiding under the covers, but she had to be awake.

"Come on," I said. "We're going detecting."

Tessa said something that sounded like "muffle muffle" and didn't move.

I decided to use psychology. "Tessa, there might be witnesses out there, and if there are, we'll have to ask questions, and you're the only one who's good at that."

There was a pause, the covers shifted and Tessa's face appeared. "Really, Cammie?"

Score one for psychology. "Get dressed, put on your detecting hat and let's go."

On our way outside, we stopped by the family kitchen for supplies. Granny was there, drinking a cup of coffee and reading the paper. You should have seen the look on her face when all five of us walked in scrubbed and dressed and everything at seven-thirty on a Sunday morning! Hooligan was surprised, too. He had been napping under the kitchen table, but the second he heard us, he scrambled out and wagged his tail.

I think Granny liked our get-up-and-go. There were Secret Service people posted on the grounds like always, so she approved our expedition provided we agreed to come back in time to dress for church. Then she gave us each a cinnamon-raisin bagel and said good luck.

"Oh—and if you can keep him under control, you can take Hooligan." She handed me his leash. "Mr. Ng won't be here to walk him till nine. But promise you'll hold on tight to his leash. We don't want any more trouble."

I promised.

Outside, the sun was up, but it was still cool, and the dew on the grass soaked my sneakers.

"Are you feeling better today, Dalton?" I asked as we walked toward the dig site.

"Uh-huh," he muttered, but he wasn't very convincing.

Hooligan, on the other hand, was feeling great. He tugged on his leash, and I tugged back. Then I tried using a command from Canine Class to see if he'd remember: "Hooligan, *heel!*"

First Hooligan looked at me like he couldn't believe

I was serious. Then, amazingly, he obeyed—slowed down and started trotting politely beside me. I told him he was a good dog, and he held his head a little higher.

As we approached the dig site, we saw it wasn't only the Secret Service and us who were up early.

Standing just inside the dig's taped-off boundaries was Mr. Golley, the head White House groundskeeper. When we stopped to talk to him, Hooligan sat down on my left, exactly the way he learned in Canine Class.

"How come you're out here, Mr. Golley?" Tessa asked.

Mr. Golley nodded at the ground. "I think we've got a guest out here, a mole. Sometimes they're awful hard on a lawn, not to mention the flowers and shrubbery."

I had a sudden thought. "Wait a second. One of Professor Mudd's students found a bunch of holes out here yesterday. Could a mole have dug them?"

Mr. Golley shook his head. "Moles most of the time dig up from under, not down from above. You've heard of a molehill, right?"

While Mr. Golley explained about moles, Hooligan was on high alert—nose up and quivering like the wind carried some special doggy deliciousness. I should've predicted what was coming and braced myself, but I was paying attention to Mr. Golley.

Silly me.

Because five seconds later, Hooligan forgot he was a good dog and did his frenzy thing: lunged forward, thumped his paws, sprang high in the air and spun so fast he turned blurry.

You can imagine what all this did to the leash attached to his collar, my arm attached to the leash, and my body attached to my arm. Tangled and tripped, I fell, and—grabbing for assistance—brought Tessa and Dalton down with me.

Ouch, ouch, and *owieee!* But that wasn't the worst part. The worst part was that the leash slipped from my grasp, and Granny was going to kill me.

CHAPTER SIXTEEN

FREE at last, Hooligan zeroed in on the hedge where yesterday we'd seen the waddling cat disappear.

Uh-oh.

With a big head start, the cat had been able to out-run Pickles. But Hooligan's legs are a whole lot longer than Pickles's, not to mention Hooligan's jaws are a whole lot bigger. If Hooligan got wind of the fat cat, we would probably be witnessing fat-cat-snack.

Time to mount a feline rescue!

Nate, Zach and Mr. Golley took off, and as soon as I was back on my feet, I followed at full speed. Behind us came Dalton and Tessa, both waving their arms like Hooligan might understand sign language, except he doesn't, so all that waving just added commotion.

We were closing the gap a few strides from the hedge when Hooligan abruptly changed course.

Did he hear what I heard—something growling from the bushes?

Whatever the reason, Hooligan all of a sudden hung a U-y and circled back in the direction of the canopy.

Trying to cut him off, I made a sharp turn, too. Meanwhile, Mr. Golley went right, and Nate and Zach left. Next thing you know, all us kids and Mr. Golley were running in breathless circles that probably looked like NASCAR—only on foot and more prone to pile up and collision.

I guess Hooligan himself thought it was good entertainment, too, because he sat down panting to spectate, which was when—"Bad dog!"—I finally managed to tackle him.

A second later, Tessa caught up with us. "No, he's *not* a bad dog, are you, puppy?" She scratched behind his ears, while I got back on my feet and tried to sort out the tangled leash.

What had happened to the cat? Was it the cat that growled?

Anyway, I guessed it was safe for now.

Meanwhile, Mr. Golley, Nate, Zach and Dalton had all come running from different directions.

Mr. Golley caught his breath and shook his head. "I'm afraid 'bad dog' pretty much sums it up," he said. "Have you seen all the holes your canine dug around here yesterday?"

It was a second before that sank in; then Nate said, "You mean it was Hooligan who was digging for treasure yesterday afternoon?"

Mr. Golley laughed. "For treasure? Not hardly. More like greasy grimy mole guts."

Tessa said, *"Ewwwww!"*

And Zach said, "There goes our million-dollar reward."

I tried to defend my dog. "Hooligan never dug a bunch of holes in the lawn before! How do you know for sure—?"

But before I could finish the question, a dirt clod smacked my shin, then another, then another, and—*"Hey, what...?" "Get out of the way!" "Stop!"*—we were all jumping back and shielding ourselves, trying to avoid the sudden eruption of splattering dirt, grass and mud caused by Hooligan, world-champion hole digger.

Thinking fast, Dalton pulled a bag of jelly beans from his pants pocket. "Hooligan, look here, buddy—treats!"

Granny's right that jelly beans are unhealthy, but I was grateful because they're also effective. Instantly, Hooligan gave up digging to snarf a dozen right out of Dalton's hand.

Some other junk had dropped out of Dalton's pocket when the jelly beans did, pink plastic things. Dalton either didn't see or didn't care, but I bent down, picked them up and stuffed them into my back pocket. We were in enough trouble with Mr. Golley already, and he can't stand litter on the White House grounds.

By then it was eight a.m., and Zach and Dalton had to leave because they'd promised their parents they'd be back early. We all would have gone, except I saw Professor Mudd busy at his desk under the canopy. Somebody really had to tell him about Hooligan and the holes.

I nominated Mr. Golley.

"Please?" I said, and tried to smile sweetly the way Tessa does.

But Mr. Golley shook his head. "That professor fellow scares me," he said. "Besides which, I've got a mole to catch."

So much for smiling sweetly. Next I looked at Tessa and Nate, hoping maybe one of them would volunteer.

But they didn't.

"Oh, *fine*," I said. "I'll do it. Come on."

CHAPTER SEVENTEEN

AS we approached the office under the canopy, Professor Mudd was sitting in front of his computer with his back to us. On the screen were numbers and dollar signs. We could tell he was concentrating, so we tried to be quiet, and I guess we succeeded, because he jumped when I tapped him on the shoulder.

Then he swiveled around, looked at us and scowled.

I was so eager to get this over with that I started right in, didn't even say good morning. "We're really sorry," I said, and then I explained. All the time, Hooligan sat next to me on his leash wearing his most innocent and sincere expression, like he had never dug a hole in his life, like the dog I was talking about was some totally different dog.

The problem was all that dirt on his paws and muzzle. It kind of gave him away.

Eventually, I ran out of apologies, and then it was quiet for a second, and then Professor Mudd shook his head and opened his mouth, and I thought, *Oh, no—we're in for it now!*

But instead of chewing us out, he showed his teeth and laughed.

"So you want to be an honorary shovelbum, do you?" He scratched Hooligan behind the ears. "I thought we had a case of canine excavation as soon as I saw the holes myself yesterday. There's no real harm done. A lot of that section we'll dig up ourselves soon enough."

What a relief! Nate, Tessa and I all exhaled at the same time, and after that it would have been "See you later," except Nate elbowed me. I looked up and saw Wen Fei and Stephanie coming toward us from the West Gate. Were they still mad at Professor Mudd? They didn't act like it; they smiled and said good morning. Then, while Stephanie petted Hooligan, Professor Mudd explained how Hooligan had done some digging of his own.

Meanwhile, Tessa straightened her detecting hat. We had solved one mystery—who had dug the holes. But we still didn't know what had happened to the gold...if there ever was any gold.

"Would you guys mind if I asked you a few questions?" Tessa asked Wen Fei and Stephanie.

The two students looked at each other, then at Professor Mudd.

"Does this have anything to do with the so-called gold?" Professor Mudd asked Tessa.

Tessa answered honestly. "Yes."

I thought Professor Mudd might get mad again, but

he just nodded. "Then it's a good thing the girls and I have already discussed it."

Wen Fei gave Professor Mudd a hard look and repeated, *"Girls?"*

Professor Mudd rolled his eyes. "Pardon me," he said. "I meant the *women* and I have discussed it. And as far as I'm concerned, you are free to answer any questions."

Wen Fei nodded. "Come on, Tessa. We can talk over here."

We all headed for the tool cabinet. On the way, Stephanie mentioned my find from the day before. In all the excitement about gold, I had pretty much forgotten it, but she hadn't.

"I have a suspicion about what it is, but I haven't confirmed it yet," she said.

"I should be able to tell you later this afternoon."

While Wen Fei and Stephanie got out their tools, I got out my notebook and pen. Then Tessa crossed her arms over her chest.

"Wen Fei and Stephanie," she began, "where did you go yesterday afternoon after you told everybody about the gold and no one believed you? Did you figure since it didn't really exist, it was okay to steal it for yourselves and hide it?"

Nate cringed and said, "Nice."

Wen Fei sniffed and looked offended.

Stephanie giggled. "No, sweetie, we didn't steal anything." She pulled her gloves on. "Although I admit stealing gold might be tempting for us poor, starving students."

"And as for where we went," Wen Fei said, "that was to the computer lab at the university. Professor Mudd asked us to double-check our results on their supercomputer."

Nate asked, "What did you find out?"

"Hey." Tessa gave him a Granny look. "I'm the one that asks the questions, remember?" She turned to Wen Fei. "What did you find out?"

"Same results," Wen Fei said. "A small piece of gold located at the northwest corner of the excavation site."

Tessa asked the question we were all thinking. "So do you know where the gold is now?"

Wen Fei pulled on her gloves, then looked at Tessa. "*We* have no idea," she said. "Do you think maybe you should ask your dog?"

It was getting late, so we thanked Wen Fei and Stephanie and started walking back to the White House to get ready for church. On the way, Tessa asked, "Wen Fei and Stephanie are still our prime suspects, right?"

"Maybe," Nate said. "But did you guys see what Professor Mudd had on his computer screen just now?"

We hadn't.

"I'm not entirely sure, but it looked like a letter asking someone to give him a lot of money for his research," Nate explained. "Do you think he's broke?"

"If that's true, he could be saying there's no gold just to throw us off the track," I said. "He could want it for himself to pay for his research."

"Or how about this?" Tessa said. "Stephanie and Wen Fei are starving students. They could definitely use a coin that's worth a million."

"I'm not so sure about that, though," I said. "I mean, it makes sense that they went to the university to check the data on the big computer yesterday."

Tessa looked like she wanted to argue, but she didn't have a chance. By now we were at the Dip Room awning, where Mr. Ng was waiting. Delighted, Hooligan tried to jump up and give his pal a big doggy kiss, but Mr. Ng knows Hooligan too well and dodged.

"He's a little bit overexcited owing to sugar," Nate apologized. "He had a few jelly beans. It was an emergency."

Mr. Ng took the leash and nodded. "Before I got this job, I could not have imagined a jelly bean emergency. Now it makes perfect sense."

CHAPTER EIGHTEEN

GRANNY used to come with us to our church, which is near Dupont Circle. But since she and Mr. Bryant got together, she's been going to church with him. Like Mr. Bryant, most of the people who worship there are African-American. Granny says she likes the services because they're lively.

But I like our church. The stained-glass windows are pretty. We get to sing. And in the boring parts, I have time to think.

That morning, I had a lot to think about. In fact, without exactly intending to, I started adding to the list of what we knew about the case. I couldn't very well write anything down with Mom sitting next to me. So I made the list in my head and tried to be logical, thinking of each new item in the order we had found it out.

- *Old gold coin could be worth a million dollars.*
- *Hooligan dug holes at the dig site Friday afternoon (probably looking for a mole).*

- *Wen Fei and Stephanie say they were at university Saturday afternoon checking data on supercomputer.*
- *Supercomputer also says there's gold.*
- *Wen Fei and Stephanie are starving students.*
- *Professor Mudd's project needs money?*

So far, I had been thinking at the same time I was standing up and sitting down and saying responses with the rest of the congregation. When the pastor stood up to give the sermon, I could finally sit still and concentrate.

Right away I thought of what Granny had told us about how important unusual stuff could be—even if it didn't seem related.

So I added:

- *Tessa acting goofy lately.*
  - *1) totally tore room apart looking for piggy bank with two dollars and 12 cents in it.*
  - *2) accused Nate and me of "interrogating" her about watching Hooligan so Mr. Bryant could play tennis with Granny on Friday afternoon.*

Wait a sec—Tessa was watching Hooligan on Friday afternoon?

Hadn't Hooligan dug the holes Friday afternoon? And hadn't we figured out that the gold must have disappeared Friday afternoon, too?

I guessed Tessa hadn't been doing a very good job of watching Hooligan if she'd let him dig a bunch of holes.

Then I remembered something else that had happened on Friday afternoon. Tessa had told me she'd put some money in the piggy bank then. That was how she remembered when she'd seen her piggy bank last.

Where would Tessa have gotten money on Friday, anyway? If she had ever done any extra chores lately, I hadn't heard about them. And we get paid our allowance on Monday.

I didn't want to think what I was thinking. It was too terrible.

And right then, I didn't have to. The sermon was over. It was time to sing. The hymn was one I didn't know: "Are Ye Able?"

In hymn talk, "ye" means "you." The point of this one, as best I can figure it out, is that you shouldn't be too hard on people for not being perfect. The second part of the hymn goes:

> *Are ye able to remember,*
> *When a thief lifts up his eyes,*
> *That his pardoned soul is worthy*
> *Of a place in paradise?*

I was quiet on the drive home, and—was I imagining it?—Tessa avoided looking at me. Then, when we got back, Tessa announced she was going to the kitchen to see if Granny needed help making lunch.

Mom looked surprised. "That's very nice of you, muffin. I guess all the church on Sunday is paying off."

Not to be negative or anything, but I wasn't so sure.

"Will you be at lunch, too, Mom?" I asked.

Mom shook her head. "Working lunch in the Oval Office for me. I have to meet with Susan about that ceremony later."

Susan is one of the speechwriters. What that means is, my mom tells Susan what she wants to say in her speech, and then Susan tells my mom how to say it.

I gave my mom a kiss and went to change back into my digging clothes. I was thinking how no one had told me I had to go to the ceremony, so maybe I didn't, when I noticed Tessa's crayons and paper were still on the rug by the window.

Oh, Tessa.

Mrs. Hedges was already mad about the dirt in the sink Friday. She wasn't going to like it if crayon marked up the rug, too. Tessa didn't deserve it, but I did her a favor and gathered it all up. I wasn't trying to snoop—honest—but I couldn't help seeing what Tessa had drawn: a series of splotchy yellow circles.

Huh?

I studied the circles on my way over to my sister's desk. It took a moment before I recognized a lady in a funky hat, besides some hard-to-make-out letters and numbers.

Then, all of a sudden, three things happened at once:

The circles made sense, my terrible suspicion was confirmed, and I had to sit down.

CHAPTER NINETEEN

"GRANNY?" It was a few minutes later, and I was in the doorway to the Family Kitchen. "Could I borrow Tessa? It's kind of important."

"Are you sure you need her?" Granny smiled at my sister, who was standing at the sink. "She's awfully useful when it comes to washing grapes."

I said, "I'm sure," and Granny nodded. I bet she wondered why I looked so serious.

Back in our bedroom, I told Tessa to sit.

"Uh...maybe I could just change my clothes while you're talking to me?" she tried. "Because, uh...after lunch we have to..."

I didn't say anything, just shook my head and pointed at the chair. Tessa sat down. I stayed on my feet and crossed my arms over my chest.

"Where did the dirt in your sink Friday come from, anyway?" I asked.

Tessa opened her mouth and closed it before answering: "The South Lawn."

"Just exactly where on the South Lawn?" I asked.

She hesitated. "Over kind of by the dig site."

"And how did the dirt get from out there to in here—our bathroom?"

"Uh...it was on something," she said, "something I needed to wash off in the sink."

"And that something was...?" I asked.

Tessa looked at her feet. "I don't want to tell you."

"Unh-hunh," I said. "Tell me anyway."

Tessa sighed. "A gold coin with a lady on it, a lady in a funky hat."

"Like the one we saw at the museum?" I said. "The one that's probably worth more than a million dollars?"

"Yeah," she said, "like that one."

I had known the answers to my questions before I asked. But still—hearing Tessa say them out loud put my feelings in a jumble. And before I could sort them out, Tessa said, "Cammie, can I ask you something? What's a pardoned soul?"

It took a moment for me to realize she was talking about the hymn from church, the hymn that said even thieves can go to paradise so long as they're pardoned.

I could see why she might be curious.

"Pardoned is the same as forgiven," I said.

Tessa nodded. "And do you think to be forgiven you have to confess?"

"Totally," I said.

"Okay then," Tessa said. "In that case, I guess I better tell you what happened. But you know what? It wasn't exactly my fault—"

"Tessa—"

"—because Hooligan dug all those holes when the big fat cat distracted me—"

"—Tessa?"

"—and if I hadn't been distracted he never would've, and then I wouldn't've found the gold in one of the holes he dug and taken it because I saw it was pretty even though there was so much dirt on it. But I didn't know it was important till later when we were out at the dig site and Wen Fei and Stephanie were telling about the gold they found with their gadget. That's when my stomach started to hurt, remember?"

"I remember, but, Tessa—"

"—So anyway, I picked it up and brought it inside and washed it off and then, because I never saw one like it, I made yellow crayon rubbings—I couldn't find a gold crayon—and after that—"

"*Tessa!*"

She blinked. "What?"

"I don't think it counts as confessing unless first you admit it really was your fault."

Tessa looked surprised. "Who made that rule?"

I didn't have an answer, so I asked another question. "Why did you go and put the gold coin in your piggy bank, anyway?"

Tessa looked at me like I was crazy. "*Duh*, Cammie. Because a piggy bank is where a person keeps coins!"

"So," I said, thinking out loud, "it wasn't the two dollars and twelve cents in the piggy bank that the thief wanted. And it wasn't an antique piggy bank with pimples, either. It was a gold coin that might be worth a million dollars. In that case, the question is: Who besides you knew what was in the piggy bank?"

Tessa waved her arms the way she does. "If I knew *that*, I could've solved the case myself, Cammie! But that's just it. Nobody knew. Honest, I didn't tell a soul!"

CHAPTER TWENTY

I had one more question for my sister. "Since all along you knew where the gold was, why did you act like you thought Wen Fei and Stephanie had it?"

Tessa turned pink. "I feel bad about that," she said. "But I figured if you and Nate suspected them, you wouldn't suspect me. And then I thought I could get the gold back myself before anybody got in real trouble."

"You realize now we have to tell the grown-ups?" I said.

Tessa said, "I know," and if I'd been smart, I would have marched her to the kitchen to tell Granny right away.

Only—call me a wimp—I couldn't do that to my very own sister. So for a while she and I both sat there in our bedroom being dejected.

Then I had an idea. The piggy bank had been in Tessa's laundry hamper, right? Which meant it smelled more or less like Tessa. And since that was true...

It was a dumb idea, and it would probably never

work. But: (a) it wouldn't hurt to give it a try; and (b) it was an excuse to put off Tessa's execution.

I explained, and Tessa was so totally relieved not to have to confess right away that she said, "You're the best sister *ever*!" and gave me a big, clingy hug.

"But, Tessa"—I undid the hug—"if this doesn't work, we go to Granny. Deal?"

Tessa nodded solemnly. "Deal."

Half an hour later, full of grapes and vegetable soup, we were back in our room, this time with Hooligan. We had borrowed him from Mr. Ng.

"Okay, Cammie," Tessa said, "I'm ready! Now what do we do?"

I opened my mouth to answer...and realized I didn't know. I'd gotten the idea that we could use Hooligan to track a piggy bank that smelled like Tessa from books I've read. I mean, Hooligan has to be at least part bloodhound; Dad says he's part every kind of dog.

The thing is, what I remembered was the idea, not the details. I hadn't exactly been taking notes when I read those books.

Then I looked at Tessa and Hooligan, who were looking back at me with total faith. Since I couldn't let them down, I had only one choice: Fake it.

"What we do first is...uh, we give Hooligan something to smell that smells like the piggy bank," I said.

Tessa looked doubtful. "Like dirty laundry, you mean?"

I tried to sound confident. "Totally."

Tessa wrinkled her nose. "If you say so." She went over to her laundry hamper, opened it and pulled out the sweaty leotard, holding a teeny corner with two fingers like it was the grossest thing yet.

Hooligan didn't think the leotard was gross. He thought it was delicious—so of course he lunged for it and would have taken a big bite, except Tessa yanked it away, which for Hooligan was even better because now they were playing tug-of-war, one of his all-time favorite games.

"No, Hooligan! Bad!" Tessa cried. Trying to protect her leotard, she held it up and jumped on her bed, so of course Hooligan followed with a surprisingly graceful leap, which meant that in a second Tessa was shrieking, and they were both bouncing so the springs squeaked, and we were not only a long way from Hooligan ever sniffing out the piggy bank, we were about to get in a lot of trouble because Granny would hear the noise and come in and catch Tessa and Hooligan playing trampoline in the house.

I said, "You guys have to get down from there!"

And Tessa said, "He's gonna rip my best pink leotard, Cammie!"

And Hooligan said, *"Awh-roohr!"*, which meant he was having such a good time he hoped we could play this game every day after lunch.

I didn't know what to do. Usually, I would tackle Hooligan—but on the bed he was too high up for that. Desperate, I signaled Tessa to throw me the leotard, which she did, only I missed the catch and it landed on my head and fell down over my face so the whole world turned pink and I couldn't breathe without getting a big whiff of Tessa's two-day-old ballet sweat.

I don't know exactly what happened next because, like I said, all I could see was pinkness, but it wasn't long till the bouncing noises stopped, and then— *thump-thump*—Hooligan must've jumped off the bed, followed by—*thump*—my little sister, and while I was trying to backpedal to get out of their way, I was also untangling the leotard from my ears, and just as I finally freed myself, I tripped over the wastebasket and fell flat on my back.

Ooof.

Soon Tessa's worried face appeared above me. "Are you okay, Cammie?"

After that, it took a few minutes, but things finally settled down. And this time when Tessa held out the leotard for Hooligan to sniff, he actually did sniff.

"Gooooood puppy!" Tessa said. "Okay, Cammie. Now what?"

What I thought was: *I have no clue.*

What I said was: "Hooligan—go find!"

CHAPTER TWENTY-ONE

GRANNY uses this phrase I like, "rising to the occasion." What it means is doing something unexpectedly good exactly at the time it needs to be done. Why I'm bringing it up is, that's what Hooligan did next: He rose to the occasion.

I mean, you would've thought our dog had been tracking piggy banks since puppyhood, because right away he got to his feet, trotted to our bedroom door and said a polite little *"Woof,"* so we'd open it and let him out.

The White House is quieter on Sunday than most other days of the week, and there was no one in the Center Hall. Hooligan dropped his nose to the rug, looked back to make sure we were behind him, then turned right and trotted toward the West Sitting Hall, every once in a while sniffing either the air or the floor.

"From now on," Tessa said, "Hooligan can do all our finding for us!"

Or maybe not.

Because all of a sudden he made a hard right into the Dining Room, again dropped his nose to the rug, lunged between the chairs and under the table and came up chewing—with a gooey green spot on his muzzle.

Oh, swell. Instead of the piggy bank, he'd been tracking a lonely leftover jelly bean.

"That's no help!" I told him, and held out the leotard for him to sniff again. "*Go find!*"

For a minute, Hooligan didn't go anywhere. Instead, he sat back on his haunches and scratched his ear. I was about ready to give up on my plan altogether when he stood, shook himself all over, sniffed the air again and headed through the Family Kitchen to one of our favorite shortcuts—the narrow, twisty back staircase to the main White House kitchen on the ground floor.

Behind us I could hear Humdinger in his cage singing, "*Twee-twee-twee!*"

The stairs clanged and clattered as we ran down. Twice, Hooligan stopped and dropped his head and I almost rear-ended him. What was up with that? Had he found treats?

But there was no time to think about it. When we emerged into the kitchen, it was hot and busy with cooks making snacks for the ceremony later.

Running through—"Hello!" "Hi!" "Hello!" "*Sorry!*"— we dodged and weaved, hoping not to cause any collisions. Exiting, I heard *rattle-rattle-bang* and then a terrible crash.

Oops.

From there we went left, then right through the Dip Room, where Jeremy opened the door for us—"Thanks!"—and then we were outside. In the cooler air, Hooligan's energy came back full force, and as hard as Tessa and I ran, we couldn't keep up.

Where was he going, anyway? Was he really tracking the piggy bank, or was he on some personal mission of his own?

Whatever it was, he had a destination in mind, and when he reached it, he screeched to a halt, circled twice, sat down and howled, *"Awh-roohr!"* like he wanted us to hurry up.

Tessa got there first and grabbed Hooligan and gave him a hug—*"Good puppy!"*—which was smart, because by then he was sniffing the ground with a little too much enthusiasm. Uh-oh. If he dug another hole, Mr. Golley would never forgive him—or us.

Now I ran up, breathless. "I don't know if he's being good," I said. "It might be he's just chasing moles again." Because where we were was the same place we'd been that morning—the Mole City part of the dig site. In fact, Hooligan was sniffing around the northwest corner where Tessa had found the gold Friday. Only there wasn't any hole anymore.

Had Mr. Golley's crew filled it in?

Tessa looked at me. "Wait—are you saying my sweat smells like some kind of rodent?"

And I said, "I don't think a mole is technically a rodent. Not to mention, I don't know how one smells. What I'm really saying is, where's the piggy bank?"

Tessa pointed at the ground with her toe. "Down there. Buried. Anyway, that's what Hooligan thinks."

CHAPTER TWENTY-TWO

MR. Golley wouldn't like it if we let Hooligan dig another hole. But maybe—if we asked first—it would be okay for Tessa and me to dig one. So the two of us and Hooligan went over to the office under the canopy. Professor Mudd was there, writing notes on the computer. His eyebrows rose and fell as we explained how Hooligan had tracked Tessa's missing piggy bank. Of course, we didn't mention the gold.

I guess our story must've sounded pretty crazy, because I had to tell it twice. Tessa didn't say a word. Finally Professor Mudd said, "So you're telling me the hole has been filled in?" When I nodded, he threw up his hands. "You may as well grab a trowel from the tool cupboard," he told me, "and together we will get to the bottom of this."

By this time, the dirt had been disturbed so much that digging was easy. I knelt and cut one scoop, then another, then another, and...oh my gosh!

I saw something pink!

One more scoop, and I saw faded, flaking painted roses.

But if you're thinking, *Woot! Mystery solved!*—well, think again. Because Tessa's piggy bank had been smashed into about a hundred sharp and tiny pieces, and soon we had the whole thing—stubby snout to twisty tail.

As for the gold coin?

There was no sign of it.

And no sign of the two dollars and twelve cents, either.

Professor Mudd shook his head. "In my entire career, I've never seen pink potsherds."

"Potsherds" is pronounced "pot-shards," and Tessa wanted to know what they were. Professor Mudd explained that the word means pieces of old pottery—among the most common finds in archeology.

"Only, these potsherds don't date from long ago," I said. "They date from more like ten o'clock this morning! I mean, this spot was just a hole in the dirt when we were out here before church."

Tessa had been totally quiet, but now her detecting instincts kicked in. "Have you seen anyone suspicious out here today, Professor Mudd?" she wanted to know.

"Suspicious?" he repeated. "No. Your friends Dalton and Zach came out to work this morning while you and your cousin were at church. And Mr. Golley brought a crew by to deal with the mole damage. But I must admit, I don't understand what's going on here. Why would anyone want to bury a smashed piggy bank?"

I had to be careful answering. I was still trying to protect my sister, after all. "I guess whoever took it in the first place was hiding the evidence," I said, "only he or she didn't count on Hooligan's superior tracking skills."

Hooligan always knows when he's being praised. Now he woofed and raised his head so we could admire his profile. He would have looked pretty handsome except for the jelly bean stains on his muzzle. Where had those come from?

Meanwhile, Tessa was asking what we were supposed to do next.

"Thank Professor Mudd and return the trowel," I said. "But after that, I have no idea. I am totally confused."

"You're welcome," Professor Mudd said as we headed back toward the canopy. "And as for what you need to do next, how about talking to Stephanie? I believe she has something to give you."

We put the trowel away in the tool cupboard and found Stephanie working in one of the trenches on the far side of the canopy. She waved—"There you are!"— and pulled a tiny box from her pocket. "This is your find from the dig yesterday, Cameron."

I felt a spark of excitement. Maybe it was gold, too?

Carefully, I removed the lid. Inside, resting on a bed of cotton, was a cup-shaped, rocklike something about two inches long and an inch wide. The caked-on dirt was gone, but it was still gray and grotty-looking.

I tried not to look disappointed. After all, Stephanie had gone to a lot of trouble to clean whatever it was and put it in the box. "Great!" I smiled and nodded. "Seriously."

Stephanie giggled. "You don't even know what it is."

"Oh...well, no, I don't. But it's still great. Do *you* know what it is?"

Stephanie nodded. "I do. It's an oyster shell."

Tessa shook her head. "Can't be. We're not at the beach."

"It didn't come from the beach, at least not directly," Stephanie said. "It came from the kitchen. Oysters were a common food in the early nineteenth century, much cheaper, compared to other things, than now. Who knows? Maybe this oyster was part of a dinner Dolley Madison served at the White House."

"Cool," I said, and this time I meant it. Dolley Madison was the First Lady when the White House burned down. She's famous for a lot of things, like helping save the famous painting of George Washington from the flames, having a pet parrot and being good at giving parties.

"What happens to the oyster shell now?" I asked.

"Significant relics are kept by the university for future study," Stephanie said. "But oyster shells are pretty common in digs in this region. If you want to keep this one as a souvenir, Cameron, it's all yours."

CHAPTER TWENTY-THREE

YOU might not think so, but a girl can work up a big appetite tracking a piggy bank. So our next stop was the second-floor kitchen for a snack. On the way, we ran into Mr. Ng and handed Hooligan over.

"Good to see you, buddy," said Mr. Ng. "You know, you've got a playdate at four."

"With who?" Tessa asked.

"Pickles, Ms. Major's beagle," Mr. Ng said. "She lives over in Woodbury, and there's that dog park nearby."

Hooligan wagged his tail. He likes Pickles.

When we got to the kitchen, Nate was already there, eating a bowl of granola while Humdinger serenaded him: *"Twee-twee-twee!"*

"Is it just me, or does that bird really need some new material?" I asked.

Humdinger flapped his wings against the bars of the cage.

Tessa got up and looked in at him. "Poor birdie, she didn't mean it!" Then she tested the door latch and its twisty-tie reinforcement. "I still don't see how he got out. It's not like he can undo these with his beak."

"Maybe Mrs. Hedges opened it to give him water or something," Nate said.

"Mrs. Hedges?" I repeated. "Earth to Nate—I change the paper, and Granny gives him water."

"So you're saying someone deliberately let him out?" Nate asked.

"Crazy, right?" I shook my head. "But so's all the other stuff going on around here lately. Tessa, can we tell Nate about your piggy bank?"

Tessa frowned. "You mean *everything* about my piggy bank?"

I shrugged. "He'll find out sooner or later. Maybe he can help us."

Tessa hesitated, then said, "Oh, all right," and proceeded to confess.

This time, she didn't bother with "It's not my fault," and when she was done Nate's eyes were as round as... well, gold coins. For a few seconds it was quiet while he thought through all he had learned. After that, he must've decided he wasn't a perfect person, either, because what he said was all about the mystery: "We know the coin was in the piggy bank. So that makes it logical that the thief smashed the bank to open it, found the coin and kept it. All that's left to figure out is: Who's the thief?"

Brilliant, Nate, I thought. And at the same moment, a voice from the doorway said, "Who's *what* thief?"

Uh-oh.

It was Granny, and she was all dressed up.

No one answered, and then something lucky happened. Granny got furious at us!

"Why on earth aren't you children cleaned up yet? It's almost three-fifteen!"

"Cleaned up for what?" Nate asked.

"What do you mean, what? The Rose Garden ceremony honoring Mr. August!" she answered.

Tessa whined, "Nobody told us we have to go, and I hate ceremonies."

Sometimes Granny is exactly like Tessa—like right then, when she waved her arms dramatically. "Well, of *course* you have to go! The medal is being presented by Dr. Maynard, and he is one of your mother's oldest friends, not to mention a family friend. Get a move on, people! I want you outside ready for pictures in fifteen minutes!"

CHAPTER TWENTY-FOUR

TESSA usually takes forever to get ready for an event.

But like a dose of jet fuel, Granny's anger sped her up. Both of us were clean, dressed and buckling our shoes with five minutes to spare.

"Get your notebook, Cammie," Tessa said. "This is probably my last chance before..." She drew a finger across her neck, stuck her tongue out and dropped her head to one side.

My notebook was on my desk, and I got up to retrieve it. I guess I hadn't been exactly tidy changing my clothes earlier, because my capris were on the floor in my way. Mad at myself, I kicked them, and something fell out of the pocket.

"What's that?" Tessa pointed.

I reached down and came up with...three pink twisty ties?

Tessa's mouth fell open. *"Cameron Parks!"* she said. "My very own sister! It was *you* who let Humdinger out of his cage yesterday! And then you lied about it, too. Not to mention you're so dumb you kept the evidence."

"Tessa, you're crazy," I said. "I was right here with you when Humdinger got out, remember?"

Tessa said, "Oh, yeah. . . . So if you didn't take the pink twisties off Humdinger's cage, where did they come from?"

I had to think before I remembered picking them up that morning. I hadn't wanted Mr. Golley to get mad at us for littering. While I was explaining to Tessa, it hit me. "Wait a second. Does that mean . . . ?"

My sister and I looked at each other.

"Cammie," Tessa said slowly, "I saw that my piggy bank was gone yesterday—right after we came back from chasing Hooligan and Humdinger. Do you think that's when it disappeared?"

"Probably."

"So what if all that running around downstairs and scaring the visitors was just a whatchamacallit," she said, "you know, when somebody distracts you on purpose so they can do something bad, like for example *steal the piggy bank right out of your laundry hamper?*"

"You mean a diversion," I said, and now my brain kicked into gear. "Plus, what about this? A certain somebody showed up awfully fast in the East Room— almost like he knew in advance we'd need help catching Humdinger."

Tessa said, "Oops."

I said, "Oops what?"

"Oops, I guess that might've been my fault," she explained. "I showed a certain person some of our shortcuts around the White House."

"Like the kitchen stairs?" I said. And by now my mind was racing. "Because *that* would explain the jelly bean stains, the ones on Hooligan's face just now. He kept finding jelly beans when we were tracking. I think *somebody* must have dropped them when he was using the stairs."

For a moment the only sound was the quiet of two brains working. I don't know about Tessa, but I was feeling pretty clever.

Then my brain ran into a massive roadblock.

"Wait a sec. None of this makes any sense at all," I said.

"Why not?"

"It's the same old problem. Nobody would've stolen your piggy bank for two dollars and twelve cents. And nobody knew about the gold coin. I mean, that's what you told me before. You swore," I reminded her.

"Nobody did know!" Tessa insisted. "Except..."

"Except *what*?"

Tessa looked at her feet. "Well, except I might've told a certain braggy, annoying someone that I happened to find something really special out on the South Lawn where Hooligan had been digging," she said. "But I never said anything about gold."

I wanted to yell at my sister, but anger would only

have burned up precious time and brain cells. "So maybe this certain person wanted to know what special thing you had found?" I said. "And maybe you wouldn't tell him, and maybe he was going crazy with curiosity?"

Tessa looked at her shoes. "Well, yeah. Maybe."

"And then he would've decided to find out for himself by looking where everybody knows you hide your secret stuff—in your laundry hamper."

Tessa's shoes must have been really interesting. "Yeah. Maybe."

"So when he found your bank, he took that, and finally had to break it to get at what was inside—"

"And then"—Tessa finally looked up—"at the museum, he found out the coin was worth a million dollars and panicked and got a tummyache, same as I did when I heard Wen Fei and Stephanie tell Professor Mudd they'd found gold. But why did this someone hide the piggy bank pieces by burying them?"

"I think I know," I said. "I mean, for one thing, there was already a hole in that spot, so burying them was easy. And also, he probably thought nobody would look there. He had heard Professor Mudd tell Wen Fei and Stephanie not to waste time on that spot because there wasn't any gold. He wouldn't have known that later, after they double-checked their results, Professor Mudd changed his mind."

My sister and I looked at each other. I think we were both a little stunned by all we'd figured out. Of course, we still had one big question: Where was the gold coin now?

But we'd have to wait till later to ask. We were almost out of time.

"Come on." I stood up. "Let's take the kitchen stairs. It's the fastest way to the Rose Garden. There's somebody out there we need to talk to."

CHAPTER TWENTY-FIVE

THE Rose Garden is right outside my mom's office, the Oval Office, which is in the West Wing. You would think with the name Rose Garden it would be mostly bushes, right? But it's actually mostly lawn, which makes it convenient for holding events.

Or anyway, convenient when the weather's good. Now a warm breeze had kicked up and gray clouds were rolling in overhead.

Helping the photographer position us, Aunt Jen looked worried. "The forecast was for dry weather, but those look like thunderclouds. Tessa, that's excellent. Cameron, please don't slouch."

We had to stand next to Dalton and Zach in the pictures, but with so many people around we couldn't really talk to either of them. Then, once the pictures were done, Tessa and I had to go sit next to Nate and Granny in the front row of chairs in the audience. Because Dalton and Zach's dad was in the ceremony, they were sitting with their mom behind the podium.

There were programs on the chairs. I picked mine up and read how Dr. Maynard was presenting his old friend Mr. August with the first national medal for a contribution to numismatics. I hoped neither one of them would make a long speech. To my mind, "You rock. Here's a medal," followed by "Cool. Thanks," would be about right.

Soon everything was ready, the TV lights came on and Mom strode toward us from the Oval Office while soldiers in the color guard saluted and eight marine musicians played the president's theme song, "Hail to the Chief."

I've seen this happen pretty many times now, but still I can't help grinning and feeling proud. That's my very own mom!

At the microphone, she smiled and said, "Good afternoon, friends, honored guests and—" A clap of thunder interrupted. "Oh, dear." Mom looked at the sky. "I hope that's not a comment on my administration's monetary policy."

I only kind of understood the joke, but the reporters laughed and laughed.

Next Mom said a few things Susan must have written about coins and Mr. August and Dr. Maynard. I zoned out. It had been a tiring day for my brain already, not to mention I'd had to get up so early.

A crack of thunder jarred me awake.

Mom glanced at the sky again. "Without further ado," she said, and introduced Dr. Maynard.

"Who else felt a raindrop?" he asked. "This may be the briefest medal ceremony in history."

Tessa, Nate and I looked at each other. *Yes!*

Meanwhile, was I imagining it? Or did I hear something besides thunder—a familiar high-pitched, insistent bark? It seemed to be coming from somewhere inside the West Wing, but that didn't make sense. Pickles and Hooligan were having a playdate at a dog park, right?

Speaking quickly, Professor Maynard said nice things about Mr. August at the same time as he opened the blue velvet box that contained the medal. Then he held it up, a shiny gold disk hanging from a red-white-and-blue ribbon.

The rain began for real just as Mr. August stood up. Also, the barking got louder. And something else happened, too—something weird, and you had to be looking in the right place to see it: The first national medal for a contribution to numismatics self-destructed.

That is, the front of the shiny gold disk separated from the back and fell—so now there were two disks.

Mr. August saw what I did and reached forward so the broken part dropped into his palm. Then, naturally, he squinted at it, trying to see what in the heck he was holding. At the same time, a bolt of lightning split the sky. Around us, people jumped up and squealed and scurried for cover.

Tessa tugged my arm. "Come on!"

But I shook my head and pointed at Mr. August. Hand on heart and face pale, he had collapsed into a chair. I don't think he even realized he was getting drenched.

Tessa said, "Cammie, is he okay?"

My answer was cut off by an uproar from the West Wing walkway. Something had alarmed the people there, who started to scoot and scatter and shriek. My brain took a second to sort out the picture—but then I saw it: a wild and furry something that shot like a cannonball through an open door.

Check that. There were *two* cannonballs, together packing two times the destructive power: Pickles and Hooligan.

CHAPTER TWENTY-SIX

CONFRONTING a looming canine threat, the few people remaining in the Rose Garden scattered like rabbits. Screaming rabbits.

But not Mr. August. He just sat staring at the gold disk in his palm.

I started toward him, but someone else got there first. It was the only other person in the world who knew it made perfect sense for Mr. August to be in shock. I mean, wouldn't you be in shock if a historic gold coin worth a million dollars appeared out of nowhere and fell into your hand?

The person shook Mr. August's shoulder, and said something, and finally Mr. August went with him to shelter under the cover of the walkway outside the West Wing.

At the same time, Jeremy and Malik ran up to Tessa and me with umbrellas.

We both ducked under and said, "Thanks." Then Tessa shook her sodden hair the way a dog does.

"Hey, I already took a shower today," said Jeremy. "Honestly, don't you two know enough to get out of the rain?"

"Sorry," Tessa said meekly.

"We'll explain later," I said, "but now we've got to find the dogs! Pickles is afraid of thunder."

"We noticed," said Malik.

"But where did they go?" I asked.

Jeremy and Malik didn't know, and neither did Mr. Ng when we found him pacing on the walkway. He told us the doggy playdate had moved here from the dog park because Ms. Major had been called in at the last minute to set up an interview. Then, with the storm so sudden, there hadn't been time to corral Pickles and close him in his crate.

"That poor dog!" Mr. Ng shook his head. "He just about went psycho on me!"

Secret Service people are posted all over the White House grounds, so Malik got on his radio to ask if anyone had seen either Hooligan or his psycho beagle friend.

There was a burst of static; then a voice reported that the dogs had been spotted near the hedge between the Rose Garden and the dig site. Did we want someone to investigate?

Tessa yelled so Malik's radio would hear: "That's a negative!" And then she turned to me. "Come on, Cammie! Fireball and Fussbudget to the rescue!"

I blinked. "Seriously?"

"We have to!" she urged. "Ms. Major's busy, and

anybody he doesn't know will scare poor Pickles even more!"

Tessa didn't wait for me to answer. She just took off running, and what was I supposed to do? I ran after her. Behind me came Malik and Jeremy, still trying to protect us with umbrellas.

CHAPTER TWENTY-SEVEN

THE dogs were easy to find. All we did was follow the path of destruction: toppled chairs, trampled plants and finally—in the same hedge the fat cat used for a hideout—twigs and broken branches scattered everywhere.

By now we were so wet it didn't matter, so we got down on our hands and knees to peer into the green darkness. Right away we saw the dogs and smelled their stinky wetness—*ewwwww*. Hooligan wore his usual nice-to-see-you grin, but Pickles was trembling and panting.

The two of them were wedged into a tiny space, their bright eyes peering back at us. It was a second before we realized there was something else back there, too—something making unhappy little "I'm wet!" squeaky sounds.

Kittens!

One, two, three, four, five... and their mama, the fat cat, who wasn't quite as fat as before.

Now we knew why Hooligan had been so interested in this part of the grounds. It was more than mole guts he wanted.

"*Awwww*, Cammie, look!" Tessa said. "But won't the dogs hurt them?"

"Guess not," I said. "Hooligan seems to think they're little buddies."

"*Woot!* Then we can keep them!" Tessa said.

"We gotta talk to Granny, not to mention Mom and Dad," I said. "But we can't leave them here. It's too wet. They'll get sick."

By now the rain had stopped and the sun was peeking through a hole in the clouds. While Malik radioed for someone to come and retrieve the cats, Tessa and I coaxed the dogs. Hooligan came out wagging his tail and grinning. Pickles was right behind him. I think he was embarrassed. After he shook the rain off, he tried to act cool, like all the time he'd thought thunder was no big deal.

The reception for Mr. August had been moved from the Rose Garden to the Blue Room. The snacks were going to be good, but the Blue Room is the fanciest room in the White House, and Tessa and I were too wet and muddy to go straight there.

Also, we needed to have a serious talk with one of our houseguests. So we took a detour to the third floor. We were pretty sure we'd find him there, hiding out.

Tessa knocked on the door to the guest suite. "You have to let us in, you know."

"Do not," said a voice.

"Do, *too*," said Tessa.

"Do not!" said the voice.

I said, "Don't you guys ever give it a rest?" and opened the door. Inside, Dalton sat on one of the two beds. He was wearing earbuds and playing a game.

I closed the door behind us, and Tessa folded her arms across her chest. "We only have one question."

Dalton took out his earbuds. "Wait...what?"

"We know you let Humdinger out so you could steal the piggy bank," Tessa said. "And we know you tried to hide the evidence by burying the piggy bank pieces at the dig site. But how did the gold coin get into the box with the medal?"

Dalton must not have been surprised we knew he was the thief. "I'm sorry about your piggy bank," he said. "And I'll pay you back the two dollars and twelve cents."

"Just answer the question," Tessa said.

Dalton sighed. "After I found out that old gold coin was worth a million dollars and everything, I didn't want it, and I thought the best place for it would be the museum where all the other coins are. I knew Dad was giving that medal to Mr. August, and I knew Mr. August works at the museum, so..." He shrugged. "Then I saw the coin and the medal were close to the same size, so I taped them together."

The scary thing was that when Dalton said this, it kind of made sense. "And you didn't think he'd find the gold coin right away?" I said.

Dalton nodded. "I thought we'd be safe back home by the time he did. I guess Scotch tape doesn't work that good in the rain."

Tessa said, "You know you have to tell the grown-ups," which was pretty funny coming from her. I mean, she still hadn't told anybody except me and Nate how she'd taken the coin in the first place.

But Dalton surprised us both. "I already did. When Mr. August was sitting out in the storm? I felt so bad for him, I explained."

Tessa turned pale. "Wait a sec. You told him how you found the coin in my piggy bank?"

Dalton shook his head. "I just told him I found the coin. He was still kind of in shock, and everybody was hurrying him so much...he didn't ask where. Then I told Mom I didn't feel good and came up here."

Tessa was surprised. "Thank you," she said. "It was nice of you to protect me. But it won't matter in the end. They're gonna find out, and then..." She drew her finger across her throat.

"Yeah." Dalton did the same thing. "Me, too."

The knock on the door made us all jump. But it was only Nate. "You guys, everybody's looking for you. They've called a press conference. Everybody knows how you found a historic gold coin out at the dig site, and now you're gonna be some kind of national heroes!"

CHAPTER TWENTY-EIGHT

I was not any kind of national hero.

Only Tessa and Dalton were... oh, yeah, and Hooligan because he was the one who dug up the coin.

It turned out that while Tessa and I were chasing the dogs, a couple of the TV guys were reviewing their video footage from the ceremony. On it, they saw the medal self-destructing. When they asked Ms. Major what was up with that, Ms. Major asked Aunt Jen, and Aunt Jen asked a bunch of people what they knew, including Mr. August and Nate.

From what everybody told her, she put together for herself pretty much what must have happened with the coin and the piggy bank and the medal.

Aunt Jen is smart.

After that, she told Mom, and Mom said they had to call a press conference right away to explain. Otherwise, the reporters would make guesses about what had happened, and with the coin being worth so much money, that might look bad.

The press conference was in the White House Briefing Room, which is in the West Wing. Ms. Major spoke first, and said that a valuable and potentially significant archeological relic had been found on the White House grounds. Then she introduced Professor Maynard and Professor Mudd, who displayed the 1796 no stars quarter eagle and explained about its potential value and historical importance.

On TV was the first time I got to see the coin close-up, and it was beautiful. I was glad that one day soon I'd be able to visit it at the museum.

After that, Ms. Major said it was Hooligan who dug the coin up in the first place, Tessa who cleaned and identified it and Dalton who came up with a "charming and distinctive means" of donating it to the Smithsonian collection by putting it in the box with the medal.

"The children will not be taking questions," she said. "We will issue a more detailed statement tomorrow."

All the cameras turned to Tessa, who waved and smiled, and Dalton, who looked scared. It was Hooligan—as usual—who stole the show. He sat straight, showed his handsome profile, wore a noble expression and uttered a single, dignified *"Woof."*

Tessa and Dalton might have been national heroes, but at home they were in big trouble. Dalton's parents took away candy for a month. And Tessa had a new chore—an especially yucky one.

"It's gonna be so worth it, though," she told me

that night as we got ready for bed. "Because they're so adorable!"

I agreed they were adorable. Not to mention furry. "But I hope you still think your new chore is worth it when they start growing up," I said. "Six cats use a lot of kitty litter."

I had one last thing to do before Mom came in to say good night. The oyster shell I had found at the dig site was still in its box. I took it out and set it on my dresser where I could admire it. I remembered how Dr. Maynard had told us shells used to be used as money sometimes. So in a way, I had found my own old coin at the dig site—one I was going to get to keep.

"Maybe I'll be an archeologist when I grow up," I told Tessa.

"I thought you were going to be a lawyer," she said, "like Mom and Granny."

I climbed into bed. "I'm not sure," I said. "Now I think being an archeologist would be okay. I'm patient, and I don't mind dirt. Plus, the work an archeologist does is a little like solving mysteries. And solving mysteries is something I'm good at."

AFTERWORD

RESEARCH is one of the fun things authors do, even authors who write fiction. For *The Case of the Piggy Bank Thief*, I not only read articles and books about money and coins, I also visited the National Numismatic Collection. It's part of the Smithsonian Institution and is at the National Museum of American History in Washington, DC.

"Numismatic," by the way, means relating to coins, money or medals.

In the book, Cameron, Tessa and Nate take the elevator to the fifth floor of the museum, and I did the same thing. There, curator Karen Lee showed me the electronically secured vault in which the nation's coin collection, one of the world's largest, is stored. Then Karen and I sat down with grad student Evan Cooney at a table in the library. Wearing gloves and using the special jeweler's magnifier known as a loupe, I examined several rare coins, including a 1796 no stars quarter eagle like the one mentioned in the book.

A visit to the National Museum of American History is always worthwhile, but you don't have to go there to see the National Numismatic Collection. In fact, if you did, you might be disappointed. Only a tiny portion of it is on exhibit at any one time. Luckily, a good place to tour the highlights is on any available computer screen at americanhistory.si.edu/collections/numismatics/.

Online, you can see and read about some of the collection's half million coins and medals, as well as its million-plus pieces of paper money. Included are some of the oldest known coins, which were made in ancient Greece, as well as beads, Native American wampum (customized seashells), teeth, nails and other items that people through history have used as money.

Some interesting items in the American part of the collection are a set of checks with presidential signatures, and two 1933 double eagle twenty-dollar gold pieces, arguably the world's most valuable coins. Only three are known to exist, and the last time one sold at auction, it brought more than $7 million!

The person in charge of the National Numismatic Collection is Dr. Richard G. Doty, who was sitting behind a desk in his messy office looking rather imposing on the day I visited. In his chapter of the book *Money of the World: Coins That Made History* (Whitman, 2007), Dr. Doty perfectly explains why a nation's coins and bills are so important to it: "... [M]oney tells the folks at home and the world at large that the regime or nation exists, that it's a going concern, and that it has the right to prosper and grow. . . . Early money proclaimed identity quite as much as it fostered commerce."

The founding fathers of the United States saw it that way, too, which is why in 1792 Congress enacted a law that established basic policies for dealing with money as well as providing for the first mint, which is a factory for manufacturing coins.

According to the new law, the basic monetary unit would be called the dollar, and it would have the same value as a coin that had been in use in America for two hundred years already, the Spanish piece of eight. The law also dictated that the dollar would be divided decimally into dimes and cents. That might sound like an obvious way to do things, but actually, it was unusual. While the idea of decimally based coinage had been around since ancient Greece, the United States was the first to adopt it on a wide scale and then stick with it.

The secretary of the treasury at the time was Alexander Hamilton. He and his allies were hoping the United States would become what's called a hard-money country, one that uses coins instead of paper bills. There were several economic and political reasons to try this. For example, at the time, coins were considered more reliable and stable than paper because each coin had the same value as the metal of which it was made.

In spite of Hamilton's efforts, though, the hard-money idea never totally caught on. One reason was that metal was scarce. Today's United States has lots of mineral resources, but in 1792 few had been identified.

Ultimately, to make up for the metal shortage, banks and other organizations issued their own notes to serve as small change. Meanwhile, foreign gold and silver coins were used for bigger transactions. In fact, a lot of early U.S. coins were actually made from foreign coins, such as British sovereigns that had been melted down.

As for the mint, it was built in the fall of 1792 in what was then the nation's capital, Philadelphia. Making a coin is not necessarily a high-tech operation. After all, at the time of the American Revolution, people had been doing it for more than two thousand years already. The process starts with rolling hot metal into sheets of the specified thickness. These sheets are cut into shapes called planchets or blanks; then a stamp called a die is used to impress an image on each side, the obverse and the reverse.

Since the coining press at the first U.S. mint was operated by hand, making those early coins took a while. As of spring 1793, the mint had produced 11,178 copper cents, and it would be five years before it manufactured its first million coins. Just for comparison, today it takes about twenty-two hours for the mint—still located in Philadelphia—to produce a million coins.

Besides establishing the dollar as a basic unit, the 1792 law established three denominations of gold coin: the eagle ($10), half eagle ($5) and quarter eagle ($2.50). However, since the average adult in the new United States earned less than $2.50 per week, there wasn't much demand for any of these high-value coins. For that reason—and because so little gold was available—it was 1796 before any quarter eagles were made.

The quarter eagle that figures in *The Case of the Piggy Bank Thief* is unique—the only coin of the time without stars on the obverse (front side). Designed by Robert Scot, the mint's chief engraver, it pictures Miss Liberty wearing a style of cap that has symbolized liberty since Roman times. On the reverse is an eagle surrounded by the words "United States of America." A total of 963 no stars quarter eagles were struck, and an additional 432 with stars.

Why two versions of the same coin? No one knows!

It could simply be that the punch that engraved the stars got broken. It could be that the stars were intended to represent states and, given that new states were in the process of being added to the union, the engravers didn't want to risk getting the number wrong. Whatever the reason behind the mystery, the no stars quarter eagle is now one of the world's most valuable eighteenth-century gold coins.

Here is a true confession. Until I did the research for this book, I thought about coins mainly when I was fumbling for quarters for the parking meter. As I said earlier, though, research is fun—plus, it almost always gives a person a new appreciation for a subject.

When I visited the National Museum of American History, Evan Cooney told me he has been collecting coins since he was in kindergarten. As he opened the boxes to show me a few of the world's rarest and most historic coins, he literally trembled with excitement. And his enthusiasm was contagious.

Now that I know a little about coins myself, I see them as pieces of art and pieces of history. Just like the First Kids, I think it's pretty cool that any old time I reach into my pocket, I might find buried treasure.

—M. A. F.